ECHOES IN THE VOID

SILENT SENTINELS DUET

RAVEN HUSH

First Edition

Cover by Crimson Phoenix Creations

PAPERBACK ISBN 978-1-923471-04-7

EBOOK ISBN 978-1-923471-03-0

wish upon a fallen star

PROLOGUE

DOLION

A tiny voice speaks to me, the sweet sounds rippling through my stone state. Even my bones ache, but I've been in this form for ... how long now, months? A year? Eyes too filled with grit peer hazily into a garden where Gisella plays with a child who resembles both herself and her husband, Sebastian, though the vampire won't come out to play in the sunlight that warms my stone facade.

But *she* isn't here, and so I let my eyes drift shut, blocking out the light, and the warmth and all the kind sweet things this world offers. Without my Minette, there is no purpose to this place. And so I shut myself away.

Soft sounds swirl around me. My stone crumbles as I strain to open my eyes, knowing over a decade or more has passed since I last emerged into this world that I hope has long forgotten me. But these are not happy sounds. These are sounds that I remember from the night when I lost her. The night I held Minette in my arms, her blood coating my hands. Even then, as I carried her from that burning hell of ash and smoke and ruin of Sebastian's house, and buried her bones beneath the earth, my skin took on its stone hue. And as my heart broke, I knew it would be a long time before I could return.

Now, apparently, I am ready. Perhaps my mind forgot to tell my heart.

The muted noises that reach me as I wake, however, are far from sweet. Tears track a face I vaguely remember. Perhaps I haven't slept for as long as I thought, and I am still in that hellish night when we fought the demoness who held my best friend's soul in her gnarled, ancient hands for so long, tortured his wife and family and destroyed my own chance at love? But no, that can't be right. Since then I've seen Gisella grow. She, somehow, managed to mother a child with her husband—a daylight miracle for the nightwalker who has been so sure his soul withered many centuries ago, yet she alone gave him light.

No, this is not that same torturous night when my own heart turned to stone. Too much has changed since then. Gisella and Sebastian's family grew, and now the love of my best friend cries.

"What is wrong, my friend's wife?" I rasp. My throat, so used to its stone state, cracks painfully. A little of my essence crumbles away. Not that it matters. Nothing about me matters after losing my Minette.

The sobbing ceases. "I am no wife," whispers a voice almost as raw as mine.

I frown. "I am sorry, Gisella. It has been an eon since I last spoke. I am....long removed from your world."

Too long, perhaps. I should have woken earlier.

I am no wife.

My gut, reforming into its fleshy state from my gargoyle form, clenches down on a diet of rock for the past however long I have rested as urgency grips me. "Tell me, please. Sebastian. Is he alright?"

Silence, after the incessant sounds that roused me, blanket the courtyard where I rest like the wake I fear I have long missed.

Stone teeth bite down on my tongue, and I taste blood. Proof that I exist, even when I should not. I try again.

"Gisella, please. End my misery."

The plea I should have made the night Minette's soul departed this world along with the demoness. Perhaps, if I have lost Sebastian, I will ask her to push my stone form into the fountain where I have graced the entrance to his labyrinth for so long and let me shatter into a thousand stone shards, truly ending my existence as I cannot do for myself.

My eyes pry wider, my vision blurring before me as I peer at the slip of a woman crouched at my pedestal in a reverent, prayerful position.

No, I am unworthy of this worship while I consider the only thing a gargoyle is incapable of doing alone for himself.

Dying.

"Gisella," I whisper, hearing Minette's French accent lilt through my mind, and my gut twists afresh at the memory. "Tell me?"

Finally, the woman before me draws the faintest, shakiest breath.

"I am not Gisella. She is gone."

My stone form returns, flesh departing as my last friend has. *No more can I suffer in this life.*

A gargoyle can only exist while his heart beats on. And with the loss of another I have loved, my heart fails its next challenge and stills in a chest that weighs more than all the granite accumulated in this world.

Again, I fade even as the woman before me sobs my name.

I will not return.

A gargoyle might not choose to die by their own hand, but they can remain in stasis for near an eternity.

Perhaps, if I forget the pain of love, I can also forget how to live.

CHAPTER ONE

DOLION

Screeches and scrapes, not sobs, broke through my slumber. *Even eternal heartbreak cannot keep me from the incessant chatter of this hellish place.* Grit crumbled into my vision as I stared down at the dark head that resembled neither Gisella, nor her daughter nor the French woman my heart desired even after my decades of dreamless sleep.

"Sebastian." My world tilted on its axis as I struggled to find my flesh and failed. "Where— how long?" I strove for the right question and changed my mind halfway through a stunted thought.

"You're awake, *mon ami*." Sebastian stopped, his black hair melding with the midnight sky behind him.

No matter how long I had retreated from his

world, for it was no longer mine, at least that much had not changed about the ancient vampire. A myriad of questions swam across my mind, but still the vision of the pretty French maid who used to visit my gardens obscured everything.

"How long?" I croaked, choking on the dust that trickled down my semi-stone throat, as though my body rejected the change to my human form.

Or perhaps my more human form, for I feared my monstrous side was a permanent fixture in this hellish life.

And like his child decades ago, Sebastian ignored my plea.

"*Merde, merde.* Put him down," the vampire admonished, as though he wasn't the one who lifted me in the first place. "And the right way up. No— Yes. Like that. Don't be frightened. It's not like he's going anywhere. His legs are stone. You see? Yes. Much better." Sebastian swept longish hair from his face and beamed at me.

Like a costumed party goer at Mardi Gras. "Aren't you jovial? How. Long?" I ground stone teeth together. The sound would have rattled my bones to my soul, had I not been in my true form, and it certainly did for the men muttering around me who fortunately stayed outside of my visual range. "Answer me, you—"

Sebastian raised an eyebrow. "Look who got up on the wrong side of the fountain today."

I blinked at him. "Would your dead wife approve of that tone, or have sufficient decades passed since you buried her mortal bones beneath this garden?"

Sebastian's eyes fixed on me, cold and hard. The monster inside him flickered, and I knew that without Gisella present, my stone eternity had reduced to a mere handful of seconds.

I smiled, heartless myself and waited for the head separating blow that would end my wretched existence.

Fucking finally.

A dead hand on my shoulder settled and squeezed. A coolness seeped deep into bones that, horrifically, remembered to *feel*.

"My friend," Sebastian murmured in English. "You have suffered."

"As you haven't," I snarled. "Why are we still here?" My body shuddered as circulation resumed into tired limbs, trembling after too long in their fixed position. A ragged breath exited my lungs as I exhaled in full for the first time in, what? Years, decades?

Sebastian smiled sadly. "Centuries, my friend. Welcome to the new world. It is...not what she would have liked. I think." He shrugged and caught my weak body that was unable to stand alone. "Come to the car. I think you'll enjoy this next part."

I stared about, taking in the closely manicured lawns, the brightly clothed servants who wore their hair in short cuts, their little legs sticking out from half sized clothing. "Do you not pay the townsfolk enough to afford proper clothing?" I muttered, coughing a small shower of grit into his neck.

Sebastian laughed. "Ah, the things I can show you. Perhaps there is joy yet to be found in this world." He led me across from the fountain, away from the labyrinth that had been my home for— fuck it, I didn't care how long any more.

Wait, I did. "The year. What year is it? Eighteen hundred? Nineteen?" My brow furrowed when he stopped and stared straight ahead.

I matched the direction of his gaze and my mouth fell open. "Now that is a carriage, Sebastian."

He laughed, long and loud. "That is a limousine, Dolion, and you have slept for nigh on three hundred years."

"Did I really?" I let him slide me into the comfortable leather interior of the sleek black carriage with its gloss metal skin. "And you disturbed me after all this time? That is undignified, my friend."

Sebastian slid in beside me and called out to the man I assumed was our driver. "Indeed but today is special, stone man. Today is moving day."

"Moving to where?" I tipped my head back to stare at the house he'd rebuilt I last recalled in ashes, searching for any sign of Minette's grave.

Damnit. I should have asked.

Sebastian's peculiar coldness wrapped around my hand. "She is with you." He tapped the back of my knuckles, and released me.

I flexed stiff fingers that still held a touch of my yellowish stone color, though that faded as though his touch had called my true nature back inside myself.

"More of your swamp witch magic?" I frowned. I had few recollections of that final night apart from fire and evil, though I recalled losing many—including the bayou wolves and the witch who helped us, if *help* was the right word.

Sebastian huffed a laugh as the carriage—limousine—rolled forward, humming beneath us. "Science. Time is a wondrous thing, my friend. You will come to see its boons, I am sure. It's good to have you with me once again. I have missed talking to you."

"You're welcome." A fanatical gleam I recognized entered Sebastian's eye. "I'm glad you're with me for this trip."

I wondered how many I had missed in the last years, how long he had been alone. How he had changed in that time. Myself, also.

"You said it was moving day?" I leaned back and stretched my legs, wiggling my bare toes.

Sebastian smirked. "We need to clothe you with something more appropriate than that, my friend. You stink of..."

That night.

"...smoke," he finished.

Not that I cared to cast my mind back, only forward for this moment. Reflection could come later. "Where are we headed?"

"New Orleans. There has been a spate of fires I want to investigate. Fires that keep happening."

A laugh that I transformed into a snort left me. "What's so special about that?" Perhaps my friend had gone mad in his dotage. Hell, I could even join him.

"The fires won't go out, and they burn hotter

than all the circles of hell. Maybe a man with your talents could help," he mused.

I tipped my head to one side. "That is a fascination," I acknowledged. "But I have no interest in fighting monster kind with you, vampire."

"Perhaps." Sebastian turned away from me, staring out the darkened window, but not before the flicker of a faint smile curled his aristocratic lips. "We shall see."

"Or I can walk home," I snarked, beyond frustrated at being woken only to find my best friend recovered and playing policeman while I still ached inside, and worse, that he had expected my heartbreak.

"And scare the locals? The house is sold, Dolion. We live in the French Quarter now. Come with me, Dolion. Something impossible is hiding in the crypts. Something hurting." He leaned forward, planting his elbows on his knees.

"Something like you and me."

CHAPTER TWO

DOLION

The cramped inside of the speakeasy was made up to look like it had been around for two hundred years even though the building had only existed for twenty. Sebastian updated my vocabulary along with my wardrobe once we arrived in New Orleans and our spacious accommodations that he had organized below street level to knock out all light from his sleeping arrangements. He'd currently dressed me in pale pants that hung loose from my thighs as though my musculature had disappeared sometime in the passing centuries, though I knew it hadn't. No, the vampire had simply...over clothed me.

A lawn shirt of some description draped across

my shoulders but clung to my skin in sticky air. The one thing that hadn't changed during my deep sleep. The air here was like breathing pure water, even away from the edge of the bayou. But even I recognized the simple pleasure of a shirt that didn't itch my skin, a craft that was worth the price tag I was certain Sebastian paid for each of the garments.

The depths of my friend's pockets, it seemed, hadn't changed in three hundred years.

New Orleans, however, had.

What I recalled as a fledgling pile of goop barely out of its primordial sludge era was a full thriving city complete with enough subculture to put the biggest cities in Europe to shame. Colorful streets displayed a mishmash of culture on the outside warring for dominance while on the inside the people Sebastian introduced me to in short order were clearly defined in their own rights, well immersed in their beliefs and ways.

The city thrived despite the damage that etched its shadow beneath the stunning street front facades. The tiny whisky bar that we sat in was no stranger to this horror. Apparently, a hurricane had ripped the previous structure from its foundations and the town had rebuilt as best it could. Despite its shortcomings, the building and its overcrowded patronage of a certain caliber held a certain charm.

I perched on my bar stool next to Sebastian where he chatted with a witch disguised as a barwench—forgive me, bar*tender*—and tried to make sense of the new world and my place in it.

Or outside it.

The four walls of the speakeasy, already imbued with enough splattered alcohol and other bodily fluids that no wooden tavern should ever have acquired in the space of a mere two decades, shrank with every sip I took of my strange, pale ale. I studied the dregs that clung to the bottom of my fast warming glass as though I could read my future in them.

"You are not wearing your *gris gris*," the swamp witch/bar wench hissed, slamming another beer on the bar top before she pushed it along to her next customer. "Be more careful, Sebastian," she warned out of the corner of her mouth before her attention switched in the opposite direction. "You pay me now." She held out her hand to the man with a more imperious nature than she used on my far from favorite vampire of the moment.

The customer let out a low growl and turned his

head half way to face her. I caught a glimpse of something silvery in his gaze that lanced the side of his face almost to his neck like a shard of metal was embedded there, before he turned away, and flicked a hand out, holding a rectangular device in her direction. A *beep* later, and the witch was satisfied.

I watched the transaction with bemusement. "Your tavern is an interesting cover," I murmured, forgetting to study my ale dregs for a moment.

The witch's green and coal black gaze lit on me. Eyes that had seen a short eternity recognized the depths of time that had passed on my own, perhaps.

Or not.

Who knew what Sebastian saw when he stared into the serpentine pits, but he seemed beyond enamored with her. For my part, I was done with witches after our last encounter with one, no matter what name this one went by in this strange age. A smile twisted her carved lips as she leaned forward, her many colorful shawls draped around her like so many faded rainbows.

"People see what they want to see, stone heart," she rasped, her imperial nature of a moment before as easily discarded as one of her many outfits, I suspected. "They come here, because they can be themselves. Like you."

She nodded to where my hand gripped my glass too tightly. The finest network of spider web cracks created a mosaic on its otherwise pristine surface.

Some of my warmed beer leaked through as I hastily placed the ruined glass on the countertop. "I'm sorry."

She shrugged. "Don't pay no mind to folk like you. It's the ones who are malicious that bother us."

A hum arose around us in agreement, and I wished I'd kept my mouth shut.

"I need to leave," I murmured to Sebastian, but the vampire sat back on his low backed stool, the edges of his lips curling upward. "We heard about the fires. And the crypt."

"What crypt?" Already I'd fallen in over my head in Sebastian's strange game. Clearly, he had a history with this woman and this place that I knew nothing about. "What fires?" He had mentioned something on the journey here. I'd barely paid attention then, still studying the inside of his enormous carriage.

The vampire at my side I swore I barely recognized anymore laughed, leaning back on his barstool. "Tifa, this is Dolion."

"Ah, the gargoyle has come back to life." She thumped her chest and one of her shawls drifted from her shoulder, baring skin. Sebastian's attention wandered until she dragged the colorful material over the strap of her dress. "It is good to see Sebastian with a friend. He has been so alone."

"You make me sound like a lost puppy," Sebastian grumbled.

"But it is true." She covered his hand for a moment, and he didn't pull away.

I turned my head, unable to watch the display of affection, not ready for it. "You mentioned fires," I said sharply. "What does that have to do with us here?"

Tifa smiled, her green gaze lancing through me. "Ah, the firebird. She hides in the shadows, bursts into flame. But the fires, those hurt people. This we cannot have. Here in the supernatural community, we take care of our own. Sebastian, he helps." She shrugged. "If the fireling does not harm others, she will be left alone."

"And what fires has she set?" condensation gathered at the edges of my glass and dripped in long runs down the sides to pool around the base.

"Several around the city. One at a laundromat."

"What's a laundro—"

"And one at a school."

I didn't have to ask about that one.

"I see." I didn't have a clue what this had to do

with either Sebastian or me apart from the fact that at sometime in the last three hundred years, my friend had left off his mourning cloak and become an intolerable flirt.

"Shall I read the cards for you?" Tifa offered, withdrawing a tarot deck from inside her mass of shawls.

I shook my head, recalling the last time I saw a deck of cards in action, and the reaction from the reader. Salt stung the back of my tongue and I managed not to lurch upward from my seat, but it was a near thing.

"No, thank you for the offer." My tone remained civil, but the look I shot Sebastian was not.

He waved me down. "We shall investigate. Thank you for your help." A fresh beer appeared in front of him, and he turned to engage the man on his other side.

The witch, however, studied me. "You should tell your friend to wear the *gris gris* necklace. He's the one who isn't fireproof, unlike you." Her French lilt that sounded all sorts of wrong dropped like another of her personalities as she tipped her head to one side.

"The what?" I watched the cracks grow up the

side of the glass, a bare millimeter at a time. "Sebastian can look after himself."

She shook her head. "Not against this. I know he's fought before. This will not be the same. I have read his cards."

Visions of the sorceress, the house a burning backdrop and Minette's body as my stone heart cracked obliterated the hidden tavern as I pushed my stool away from the bar. The witch watched me as I panted, my knees stiff, heavy. *No. Not here.* I couldn't revert to my stone state in this ridiculously close space. I'd be at the mercy of whoever came alone and from what Sebastian showed me of this time and place, the people were ... .less than respectful.

Perhaps that was why he'd taken me to an inn filled with supernatural creatures where the people pretended they were from another time, pretending to be normal when they were anything but.

Because here, where my monster showed through, only my own kind would judge me.

But that was the revelation I'd had as I studied my ale dregs. There were no more of *my kind*. Not that I'd seen in 1735 when I helped Sebastian build the house. Not since I left Europe and my perch above the church in a street anchored of gargoyles and all the hideous, ugly things just like me.

And certainly I hadn't seen another creature like myself here.

I spun away from the witch, unable to bear her serpentine gaze or her strange collection of colorful personalities any longer.

In the corner of the room amidst the shadows, something brighter than any of the barwenches' shawls emerged, if only for a moment. I looked, because that's where, had I been given the choice, I would have hidden. But Sebastian dragged me to the counter upon our arrival and that was where we had stayed and he had hosted his conversation. From what I gathered, he was a regular here, in his role as supernatural sheriff.

My eye, however, was drawn to a different prize.

Hair the color of burnished copper hung to her shoulders in the sort of blunt cut that suggested a hard and stubborn exterior. That alone should have told me to stay away from the woman who glowed with an aura like the sun rising above the Caribbean on a midsummer morning, but it was her eyes that gave her away.

Those were ember black, the sort of darkness that lit a flame from within. She allowed me a rare glimpse as I met her gaze within the shadows when everyone else in the tight, crowded space ignored the girl hiding against the wall.

Bare shoulders gleamed a radiant cinnamon, different from the dark skinned peoples of the bayou I was so used to seeing, or the bar witch who still studied me with serpentine gem eyes that both suited her and didn't.

Not that Sebastian seemed to make the distinction as he leaned forward, engaging Tifa in small talk. I looked back at the shadow woman, but her corner and table sat empty. A survey of the room assured me that she'd taken my moment of distraction to escape.

"You were hiding," I muttered to myself as I walked away from the bar, leaving Sebastian to flirt —an action that still left centuries old betrayal in my mouth, though he had obviously moved on. "But who were you hiding from?"

I reached the empty table, and swept my fingers across its surface, coming up with nothing but fingertips coated in the finest, dark particles. Frowning, I raised them to my nose, and sniffed.

"It's ash, stone heart," the witch whispered in my ear.

I jerked back with an oath, but when I checked

the space beside me, Tifa still stood back at the bar, though she'd stopped speaking to Sebastian, and watched me again.

"Whenever she disappears, that's all that is left. Makes a hell of a mess." Her head tipped from side to side as she considered me and spoke in that voice that reached me across the room though she talked to no other. "Why don't you try the cemetery? The largest one. I'm sure your friend will show you the way." She gave Sebastian a prod.

He moved reluctantly off his stool as she murmured something in his ear. The vampire listened attentively, then leaned in and kissed her cheek.

I pretended not to witness their show of affection as my own heart, the organ unfortunately not stone as I wished it, pumped furiously inside my chest cavity. The betrayal I wished would stop and still in the world did no such thing, and the muscle beat on, forcing me to take breath after breath as I ignored Sebastian's after-death choices and focused on the odd pile of evidence of my strange girl before me.

Proof that she existed even if I didn't want to anymore.

Circling my fingertips in the silky ash, and leaned against the empty table, trying to work out how my strange shadow woman left the room without being seen or moving at all. I came to the conclusion I was as mad as any of the patrons in this place just as my ale glass I'd left on the bar top exploded into a thousand shattered fragments.

Glass shards littered the floor, reflecting copper highlights like the building itself couldn't forget the woman just as I could not, long after she'd gone.

CHAPTER THREE

ASH

Every time I fell in love, they died. I mean, I wasn't cruel in my intent; I died too. But their deaths were accidental. Mine, on the other hand...I knew what was coming, even if my poor lovers didn't. An occupational hazard of falling for a creature who burst into flame uncontrollably every time my emotions roused.

Hormonal imbalance didn't come close to covering it.

I curled in the top end of the shallow crypt where it stood on its stilts, the city's protection against flooding many years before, and pretended that if I ignored the man waiting outside my locked door, he would go away.

Spoilers: he didn't.

Hour after hour he waited, he and his friend. The pale, dark haired man paced. He grumbled, then lit a cigarette. I hated the smell of those, either lit or unlit. He strode around, made some drama and finally, after an argument that I couldn't tell if it was staged or not, he left, leaving me with the man who leaned against the crypt opposite mine in New Orlean's largest cemetery, standing right where he had been the whole time since he had arrived.

This man was different from his friend. Tall, and strange skinned, like a hue of unpolished wood or stone covered in lichen and left in the sun afterward too long. He had taken a tour of the graveyard walk alone, pacing every path, his fingers trailing every headstone. Then he studied the crypts, one at a time. I followed his path through the myriad of cracks in my walls, the crumbling holes in my walls offering the perfect view of his odd activities. His friend groaned in the moonlight then, too, like an incessant toddler begging to go home.

"Then go home," I murmured, watching my odd man.

His heavy set shadow remained a swatch of darkness as he wove his way along the walk that led to my crypt. One more step, then another, he drew closer and closer. And when he finally arrived—

He didn't touch the door. Only stepped a pace away and leaned his back against the obelisk opposite my crypt while I shuffled around inside my small space.

And then he waited.

I curled into the top corner and did the same, peering through the cracks in the marble as the night faded and the new dawn brought color back to the world.

And it occurred to me *why* his friend had been so vocal about their task, and why he needed to leave so abruptly.

Then I did the stupidest thing a hidden creature like me could do. Even though we both knew that I hid right in front of him, where he stood as still as stone, like he refused to move until I emerged.

Just like he had when he'd seen me in the bar. He waited.

Then, I ran.

Now, I laughed.

My hand clamped over my mouth, but it was too late—the sound tore from me in that horrible sort of high pitch that carried across the small graveyard path toward my little stalker. Because that's when I knew I'd made the worst mistake of my life.

Unlike his friend he didn't run away. He didn't even come closer.

He just closed his eyes, the faintest smile playing across his enigmatic face.

And then he turned to stone.

Suddenly I was staring at a statue of the man who appeared threatening as the sun rose over my crypt and I was left alone.

Only I wasn't.

Because even though he was no longer the threatening presence I expected, there was something strangely comforting about the man who just came to lean against the wall opposite my hiding spot, the smile that lingered on his stone face like he had been carved that way. Every detail of his yellowish, albeit granite looking stone facade was highlighted, I suspected, by the golden hues of the rising sun that flashed over his face.

I followed its path across his strange skin until it rose above the plinth behind his bald head, leaving sharp definition around his heavy set body. Even dressed in modern clothing, it was clear from his cross legged, tall pose, the way his chin tilted slightly as though he had seen so much of this world that he looked down upon everything in it that, like me, he originated from a different time.

That he had weathered the trials of this world as I had.

I wondered if he bore the same sorts of scars on his other skin in the same way as I did.

The dichotomy of my strange stalker drew me out of my hide. The daylight hours that I'd traditionally avoided for so long didn't seem quite as terrifying while he stood guard outside my tomb. Not that New Orleans was busy in the early morning. Like the rest of the city, I was most active in the evenings.

It had become easiest to hide in crowds and so I slept through the days and stirred in the late afternoon to find my place amongst the people of the current city in the night. Even so, I still didn't quite fit here, as I hadn't fit anywhere for so long.

But I'd still prefer to be an eternal stranger in a wandering crowd than alone forever, shunned and known, avoided for who I was but could never control. And because of my selfish nature, I threatened everyone in the vicinity.

Perhaps my new stone stalker friend should be scared more of me than I currently was of him rather than the other way around.

Checking the aisle in both directions like a child, I slipped into the shadow on my side of the cleared pathway, leaning my back against the cool, white stone of the crypt. The cemetery was empty just after sunrise, though on occasion an early riser would walk the paths for the same reason I chose to hide here.

Peace.

I'd encountered enough hate recently to choose my company. Even when said company took the form of a stone man stalking me. Though the silent sentinel across the path from me didn't look like the hideous gargoyles I'd often encountered in Europe during the darker years of those thriving lands. Back then, fairytales and nightmares roamed the streets during daylight hours that might as well have been dusk for all the meager sunlight that filtered through the dirty clouds that hung over those nations.

I'd seen countries change their names and flags enough times that I'd forgotten what most of them were called in this era. I would bet my last treasures that the man across from me did, too.

Standing this close, his pose looked less...forced. As though he chose to remain stone and could walk away from the wall in his current form at any moment. Checking the pathway again for newcomers and finding the aisle empty, I crept closer.

Last night I ran from him in the bar. Today, I used the sun rising at my back, hiding in its warmth and blazing fury as I studied the creature who followed me and invaded my space right back.

Of all the people who had sought me out over the years, very few found me for any pleasurable purpose. Usually, they wanted to cage or display my talents. Neither of those turned out so well for either of us. Claustrophobia was a weakness of mine. Laughable for a woman who chose to spend her days in a close space, but then, that was the operable word wasn't it? *Choice.* I *chose* to be in the crypt, not locked away.

This close to my stone man, warmth reflected back at me, but it wasn't from his own energy, rather that of the sunlight that I soaked up. He stood tall, a far more imposing figure in his loose pants that muscular thighs filed out and the casual shirt he'd worn last night. The rolled sleeves suited him, patterns that weren't quite tattoos but looked instead of whorls carved into his very skin.

I grazed my hands over the space between us, not yet daring to touch him, working my way up to that breach in his privacy. He was asleep, after all, and that felt like some breach in trust between us. But the closer I leaned into him, rising on my toes as high as I could reach to breathe across his chest, straining to reach his face, I knew the temptation would be too great.

I am too starved for human connection. Contact.

I could keep lying to myself as much as I wanted but this strange stone man who stood nearly double my own size and height, seems both powerful and strong. Strong enough to manage my deadly touch, perhaps? Or would he wither and die and ash like the rest? Not that it would matter. I'd be gone before he woke.

But surely one small touch wouldn't hurt.

Just one.

"Who do you choose to be?" I whispered, reaching up to trace my fingertips across the generous lips that seemed to soften beneath my fingertips. "What's your name, stone man?"

Golden eyes flared to life as my stone man stared down at me. "I chose to live," he murmured back.

Breath halted in my throat, the hitched inhale suppressing a scream I couldn't have kept in if I tried and so I supposed I was grateful for the horrific choking sound I made in lieu of a high pitched wail in his face at close quarters.

But the hands that manacled my wrists, large enough to engulf my forearms, were warm, despite the unyielding stone surface that didn't give against my flesh.

That I couldn't pull away from. Not that I didn't give it my best try.

"Let me go." I twisted my hands in his grip, trying not to flail and panic, but not far off it, either.

My stone man watched my struggle politely. "No."

I blinked, and stopped. "What do you mean, *no*?" I gave a half-hearted tug knowing he wouldn't let me go anyway, and stopped.

Thunk. Thunk.

Thunk. Thunk.

I leaned a little closer, angling my head.

Thunk.

"My heart works just fine after a moment to let the blood flow again," my stone-stalker said softly.

Not an ounce of aggression flowed from him, despite the fact he held me prisoner. But he didn't move, and neither did I.

"It didn't make that sound a moment ago," I blurted, refocusing on his face, where his skin changed to a bronzed glow where the yellowish stone color dropped away. "Before, you were…"

"Dead?" The corners of his lips curved, though his mouth never lost its carved quality.

I realized how close we stood, but he held me firmly in place, and I couldn't step back, even if I wanted to. And still I listened to that mesmerizing rhythm, as though every heartbeat was precious.

"Quiet." I raised my gaze to meet his amber glow in challenge.

He nodded, returning my study. "You left me in the bar. Actually, you left a little...mess."

I flushed the same color as the roots of my fire-brick hair. "That's kind of unavoidable. And rude to point out." I flicked my fingertips at his chest. That little motion had about as much effect as flicking an iceberg.

Amusement flickered behind his eyes. "That you avoided the witch and my friend speaks of no little skill. They are determined."

I wrinkled my nose. "Someone always wants something," I muttered. "Like salespeople at the door." Confusion crossed his face, and I hurried to correct my assumption of before. *He knows less of this world than I do.* "I just want to be left alone."

His features softened, though he still retained a glimmer of that inhumanity that left him looking carved and removed from the world. The impossibility of him was...intoxicating. It had been a long, long time since I stood close to anyone, let anyone touch me for fear of ending their existence. Yet this man touched me without that same dread. Refreshing, but only because he didn't realize his mortal existence was threatened with every breath of that fascinating heart of his within his body.

"I understand that need. What's your name?" His thumbs grazed across the center of my palm, stopping there to rest.

The constant contact was so intimate, breaking through my thoughts, that I couldn't concentrate on anything but the gentle strokes he made over my palms. "Stop that," I whispered, pulling back.

He let me go.

I stumbled back for a fraction of a second—long enough to hear what our conversation had obscured. Approaching voices. And not just one, but many.

I closed my eyes. "The morning grave tour." I hated them. Every second week, one of the community groups brought people through the graveyards. Educational, sure. Disturbing? Absolutely. I twisted away, but the path across the way to my hiding place to the raised crypt above the water level had never seemed so far.

A quick glance along the lane assured me the

tour group walked far too fast for an educational lesson this morning.

"They're not looking for me," my stone man echoed my thoughts.

His hand found mine before I could answer him, but this time his firm grip didn't create manacles around my wrists as he swung me back into his body. Warmth enveloped me for the briefest moment.

"What–"

"Close your eyes, Steorra," he murmured. Cool lips brushed my temple as he turned us with grace I recognized. The sort of balance and grace that only came with many miles walked upon this earth in the same form year after year after year.

Because he, too, was an ancient one.

Steorra, he called me. An ancient word for a bright burning star.

Heat travelled along my body as alarm tore through me.

Not now, not now—

Panic followed hot on its tail. "I need to run," I hissed, fighting against him, though I didn't want to.

My stone man braced his arms over my head, arching his body around me, and—

Silence fell.

Inside his arms, I shivered. The stone of him, so much more than a facade, was cold. Outside the chatter of the group continued, louder as they passed but still muffled. I held still, keeping my breath inside until my lungs were fit to burst, but no one stopped at my tomb, and no one poked that odd stone statue that had just appeared in the cemetery, unnamed and unmarked.

Apparently my stone protector looked just like any other stoner creature in New Orleans, hiding in plain sight.

Letting out my breath a whisper at a time, I pressed my cheek to his chest and rested.

Then my eyes flew open.

Nothing.

His chest might as well have been as he said before—Dead.

No sound came from within him, the stone of him complete. No breath, no heartbeat. I tried to untangle our fingers but he'd laced our hands together in a way that refused to let me escape. The tour group turned a corner after a detailed discussion on my row, and I fidgeted, tugging at my fingers.

HIs squeezed back.

I trapped my yelp between clenched teeth, forcing the sound down and managed a breath. "I am going to scream in your face one day," I muttered. "And you'll have earned the privilege."

"I look forward to it, Steorra." One hand detached from mine, and I mourned its loss as he risked raising it to trail through my hair. "You are the brightest burning star. What is your name lest I pick a constellation to name you after?"

"Wouldn't be the first time," I muttered, staring at the ground. He laughed softly, far too sexily with our bodies pressed too close in the tiny space against the obelisk opposite my crypt. My cheeks blazed even as I squeezed my eyes shut. "You may call me Ash."

He remained silent for a moment, though thick fingers played in my hair. "Ash because you consume everything, or is it short for something else?"

It's short for something. That's what I meant to come out. But my body chose that moment to over-heat and all I could think of was that I was glad to know the community group had moved on as I couldn't contain this next part at all.

My next thought was that we were about to find out how fireproof my stone man was.

"Run, run," I whispered, reaching out and squeezing his arms to hold him tight, my words clashing with my thoughts as I gave him the singular truth I could to free myself from everything that might actually keep this enigmatic man who seemed to understand me close. "Someone else sets the fires. I am not the one you seek."

He stared down at me, his yellow gaze oblique, unfathomable.

Just once, would it be so wrong to have someone be able to touch me? Someone who I can't hurt?

The impossible plea. I knew, because I'd been begging the universe for that for over three thousand years. Why would it start giving me what I wanted now?

"Run," I pleaded instead, staring up at him. "Go, now."

He smiled faintly. "No, Steorra. I will stay."

Hot tears tracked my cheeks, burning my skin even as he watched my flames burn through my skin with the sort of awe they all had in the beginning. Right before their screams began and I couldn't control anything anymore.

But this time, I didn't get to hear his screams because yet again, I was nothing more than a pile of ash in a public space, and everything around me burned.

But like every Firestarter, I would rise again.

CHAPTER FOUR

DOLION

My Steorra left me staring at a pile of ash as the woman before me disappeared in a blinding flash. Stone shielded my eyes a fraction of a second behind her disappearance, long enough to feel her heat before she died right in front of me.

Again.

This was becoming a bad habit.

My heart beat at a frantic pace the moment my skin returned to its usual color, but by then my fiery star had returned to her regular hiding spot. A deep laugh rumbled through my chest as the community group returned from their walking tour in time to see the laughing statue. Several paused in their confusion and chattered needlessly, flashing me with hand help devices.

I winced at the extra light, and swore her giggle followed the group through the cemetery even as the shape of her seared into my arms, as though she still pressed against me. I'd come so close to pressing my mouth to hers that my lips ached for the missing contact. And hot on the heels of that little misdemeanor came the deluge of guilt dressed as a different face, one from a different time framed by golden ringlets and rosy cheeks.

"Minette," I rasped, squeezing my fists tight and scaring the last of the locals who stared at me askance like I might rob them, or worse.

But the draw to the woman with the copper hair that glinted like burnished starlight in the fresh morning sun could not be ignored. *Perhaps Sebastian has it right.* A gargoyle's heart could only beat while it was whole, after all. I had slept for three hundred years waiting for my brokenness to heal after the death of my beloved. Someone once told me that time healed wounds. Perhaps in a physical sense that might be true, the simple knitting of flesh and blood. But I'd never believed it in the metaphorical space, where a mental chaos or a sickness of the heart could simply be defined as *fixed* by the series of sunsets and sunrises over my ugly, twisted shadow.

Until, perhaps, now.

I waited until we were alone, the small crowd moved along on their tour of innocuous chatter and inane facts about the lives of people they neither knew nor would remember in the next moments when they changed to the lane beyond the crypt I watched. Then I crossed the path and knocked on the wall of her stained marble tomb.

"Are you coming back out today, my Steorra?" I murmured, keeping my voice low.

Her soft breaths were the only answer I received.

Alright. She could keep on hiding. I understood that need. My lips twitched as I traced the crack I knew she peered through at me, obliterating her light source for a moment before giving it back.

"Shall I return later for you, or will you find me?" I didn't let her answer, wandering away from her crypt. She would create her own path. Something told me this girl sought her own destiny, though her words still rang in my head.

Someone else sets the fires.

I am not the one you seek.

As though she wanted to be the one I needed. Or perhaps that was a pithy fantasy my strung out heart craved in desperation for contact with another of my kind. Relief hit me that she hadn't hurt children in a school or the other place that Tifa mentioned. But she wasn't of my kind. No one here was. Of all the sorts I'd seen in the witch's tavern the night before, or the statues where today, no one was like me.

Or like her. The soft thought whispered through my mind, unbidden. I wondered if Sebastian also found himself alone, or created a hive of vampires in my tri-century long absence. The thought soured in my gut as I refocused on the task at hand.

I loved you, Minette. I love you still. And you will have all my memory and my heart of three hundred years. I pray you will forgive me in this.

My heart beat once, hard and painful and I gave into the thought of my Minette watching, and begged her mercy.

The short time I had with her was not enough. It should have been a mortal lifetime, but that was stolen by the demoness she ended, and gave her own life to free us.

"I love you," I murmured, my voice low enough that the faintest flicker of morning breeze in the still, muggy air whisked my words away. "And yet, I live." *While you do not.*

Perhaps Sebastian lived through his pain.

Perhaps I had been selfish in my solitary confinement of stone while he bore his grief alone.

Perhaps, perhaps, perhaps.

And now, a fallen star called to me. Her brightness imprinted across my chest, an ember that burned soul deep, etching herself there.

I released a fragmented breath.

No, she was not the one Sebastian hunted. Maybe Ash—not her true name, I was certain—was who I needed, however.

I am not the one you seek.

Wasn't she?

A soft laugh followed my confession, and this time the winds didn't deign to steal my sounds. All I had to do was convince my best friend of that little fact on the word of a flighty being who burst into flame and ash every moment she was scared, even though he seemed to have missed her display back at the tavern.

The witch hadn't, however.

I slipped my hand into my pocket, rubbing my fingers in the pinch of ash I kept there. I'd keep the small souvenir for myself, if for now, in any case. Perhaps Sebastian was into something with this mystery solving bent of his. It was time I joined the fray.

~

The witch's tavern that I had frequented on my arrival in New Orleans—The Devil's Fool, a play on the major arcana, Sebastian's current voodoo crush was far from my first brush with magic users—was far from full of patrons as it had been the night before. I settled at the bar while he slept back in our room, hidden below street level where light could not enter our basement level dwelling.

"The same as you had last night?" The witch, Tifa, offered. Her many shawls dragged across the bar top in her wake.

I nodded, knowing I wouldn't gain a single word of information out of her without Sebastian at my side if I didn't drop coin in return for her custom. Metaphorical coin, I'd come to understand, after reading his scrawled instructions about the phone and how to work it. I held the screen to my face, tapped the colored square—I prayed I picked the right one—and held it out gingerly in payment.

The bleep told me I got it right. Tifa's broad grin told me I didn't fool her for an instant.

"Glad you've joined the real world."

"He's spoken about me." I bit back an oath and

offered her a fake as fuck smile that bit into her good humor.

"At length." The smile slid off her handsome face. Not my style, but Sebastian and I always differed in our tastes.

Damnit, I need to keep her happy.

I toyed with the ale that she poured for me and wondered how in all the hells I was supposed to start this conversation. "Perhaps I should have ordered something a little stronger."

"Or start with what you know."

I winced. "I am...unpracticed."

Her nose wrinkled. Even that small motion had an edge of grace to it. "You don't say." She blew out a breath. Knowing emerald eyes found and held mine. "Is it about the phoenix girl The firebird?" she prompted when I didn't immediately respond to her barb.

I canted my head to one side. *Interesting assumption, and wrong.* About the girl, yes. That she was a phoenix... There, Tifa was not so correct. Not that I'd be removing that assumption from her any time soon. The longer she thought my Steorra was a firebird, the longer she might leave her alone.

Certainly, my girl's little ashing issue held some similarities, but she didn't flap her way to freedom, and she wasn't reborn in the traditional phoenix manner. I'd encountered plenty of those in my lifetime. No, Ash was something rarer than a firebird. Plus there was that little flash of light that preceded her combustible moment...

I smiled into my ale. "If I told you there was another cause of your fires in your city, would that change the trajectory of your search?"

Tifa stilled. "You have evidence that your friend will accept, of course?" She flicked idly at the tangled fringes of her many seals, the rainbow melding into a conglomerate of color. "He won't like that you've brought change to his plans."

"He'll have to get used to it," I said quietly. "It was his idea to bring me along." That Sebastian had sold the house without consulting me and interrupted my slumber still irked deeply. "I was...resting."

She snorted. "You were sulking, my friend."

A deep growl reverberated through my chest. "My heart shattered over the love of many lifetimes stripped away by the sort of demoness this world has seen only once before."

"We all have broken hearts to suffer. Do you think you are the only one to be besotted by the devil and made a fool by him?" Tifa asked softly.

I glared at her for making a pun of both her bar's

name and my plight. Minette's fate, though three hundred years had passed in these people's time, was still too fresh in my own. "How long have you been in this place?"

The witch shrugged one shoulder. Elegance exuded from every movement. I wondered if she hadn't been a dancer in her previous life. "Near fifty years. I have seen New Orleans change. Not from the muddy pilchard it was when you first arrived, the fledgling port struggling to survive when the first *filles à la cassette* arrived."

"Gisella." My heart panged at the thought of first Sebastian's wife, then her daughter. Both losses long past, like my Minette. The betrayal that I now flirted with another woman, held her in my arms, breathed her warmth in ... It grew too much.

Heat of my own burned within me. Not bright like Ash's, but a low, cold smolder of self-hatred that would never go out.

Minette. I miss you.

I loved you.

"Hell, I love you still." My voice cracked as I stared blindly at the wall behind the bar owner's head as though I could bring back the woman I had loved and lost by lack of willpower alone.

But nothing could bring her back now, and I was left with nothing.

Sebastian had moved on. He'd brought me here with the express purpose of creating a new life, and I hated him for it. For moving me from my fixed place, taking me from the garden and away from her grave where I should have rested beside her for an eternity.

Forever, as I promised her when I last turned to stone in that place.

And now I was here, living again. Fascinated with life.

It felt...right.

And yet so wrong.

Fury built within me at Sebastian's trickery as memory assailed me. The anger I'd kept inside turned on the witch hiding in plain sight right in front of me.

"Be glad she dispatched the evil so your kind don't have to ever deal with it," I snapped, slamming the base of my glass onto the counter.

Cracks formed along the sides even as I clamped my palms around the tall glass to prevent the inevitable. As it had the night before, the glass shattered, though this time it slopped its contents on the bar top.

Tifa sighed, sweeping a cloth that soon water-logged as she cleaned the remnants of my mess from the scarred wood. "That's two you owe me. I keep a tally," she reminded me.

I nodded and held out the phone.

"I'll take payment when you bring her back. The one who isn't what I think she is."

Damn bar witch.

Her laugh swirled around my head as I left The Devil's Fool, heading for our accommodation. I wanted to clean up before I sought out my strange little fallen star.

She should almost be awake by now, and despite my self loathing, and the penance I heaped upon myself, I had a promise to keep.

CHAPTER FIVE

ASH

The stone man stood outside my crypt for a second time as darkness blanketed the graveyard. And for a second time, I didn't tell him to leave.

Or flash fry him again.

He hadn't disintegrated like everyone else did when I lost my shit. That earned him significant brownie points in my book, even though I suspected he wouldn't understand the reference. Nor did I understand who he spoke to when he waited afterward, murmuring softly as though he prayed, though I didn't think he was the prayerful sort. No, we were gods amongst these mortals. Not above them in any way, but...apart.

Unlike them, as we were unlike all others.

Even his friend who seemed to have immersed himself in the culture of this world and all it had to offer. I wondered if he had always been that way, or if he, too, had struggled with a sense of time and place and where he stood within existence, once.

Or not.

Maybe one day we'd be on good enough terms for me to ask. Or maybe I'd ash him before I got the chance. Who really knew? That was the story of my intimate life right there: fall in love, have a snog, pile of ash.

My sex life, summed up in three dot points.

I'd never made it to third base, because intimacy caused that same flash/bang result my stone man experienced first-hand.

"So why aren't you ash?" I asked the inside of my crypt.

"Why don't you come out and we can work it out together?"

I started when he answered, not realizing he'd been listening so hard to my internal ruminations, as though he could read my mind all along. "It's not nice to eavesdrop," I snapped.

"It's not nice to incinerate someone when they're offering you protection," he rebuked me softly.

Amber eyes met mine through the larger cracks

in the stained marble. I swore the gaps were bigger than they had been the night prior as I crouched over the cold slab. My fingers traced the name etched into the stone that had worn away from floods the raised dais didn't protect decades before, no matter the designer's intent.

"It's a failsafe," I muttered, creeping forward, until my fingertips pressed to the outside. Another flash, a little ash, and I stood in the night air beside him, reeking of stale graves and death. "It always fails to keep me safe."

Hard, thick fingers hesitated a breath from my cheek before they made contact. His touch was warm and firm, as before, and he sought permission before his skin grazed mine. I nodded once, and didn't pull away. Because I felt like I knew this man, despite his hulking size.

And he was *safe.*

"So you're not going to ash me this time?" The corners of his mouth lifted momentarily.

I shrugged, just to let off some steam on my sassy side. "I mean, I might. If you let that stoic nature of yours come out to play. Your stone could use a little tan on the other side." I wiggled my pointer finger in a circle, indicating he should turn around like a rotisserie chicken on a skewer.

He laughed, long and full bodied. I liked that sound, and wondered what it would be like to listen at closer quarters, with my ear against that great, heavy chest of his.

"I might be a bit pasty on my other side," he conceded, wiggling his backside.

I bit back a laugh. "I'm not sure I can deal with a smiling stone man," I admitted, circling him, and checking out the goods he offered. Nothing had changed about his well over the mid-six-foot-five-inches range and brick shithouse ranking shoulders that stayed as still as he had in his stone form until I completed my inspection. I bit my lip and made my first confession since he had been nice and held to his promise of returning to see me. "I don't know your name."

"Dolion."

My lips made his name in silence as I tried it out. *He's definitely from a different time.* We had that in common. Those citrine eyes lit on me as I completed my rotation around his heavy body—not an inch of fat anywhere on him that I could fathom—and I cleared my throat as well of my mind, of filthy thoughts. Clearly, I'd been deprived of male company, or any company, really, for far too long.

"Did you need me to say it again?" His eyes

tracked my movement, tracing the shape my mouth made.

I shut my lips tight and shook my head.

His lips quirked. "In that case, I should sleep."

"Sleep?" I broke my vow a fraction of a second after making it. "But you just got here."

"And now I know that you are safe, perhaps you will return the favor. I have been awake for too many hours, and this body is...tired." He leaned against my crypt, his shoulders dropping slightly.

I frowned at his posture. "Is that a...thing?" My frown deepened when his expression matched mine, and I shook my head. "You haven't been around for a while, have you?" I murmured. *Gotta watch the references with this one.* Actually, it was kinda a breather to drop the current language with this man and drop back into an older style of speech that I hadn't used in a long time. "Let's give this a go. I might be a little rusty," I warned him, though those amber eyes never wavered in their focused gaze, despite the way he shifted restlessly against my crypt. "You need rest after being up for the day, then?" I clarified.

He nodded, leaning his head back against the marble. "I used to wake at night, roam the bayous with Sebastian. My vampire friend," he said, his voice near a thin whisper. "Back when..." Dolion's voice trailed off.

I bit my lip. *Don't pry, don't pry.* "Back when what?" I asked softly.

I am shit at this.

Dolion pried his eyes open that had fluttered shut. "Back when I was in love. Three hundred years I slept. You'd think I have had enough of wasting my own time, would you not? But no. May I perch on top of your crypt while you sleep?"

He didn't wait for an answer before slinging one long, muscular arm that strained the thin material of his fine cotton shirt over the peaked roofline of the crypt. He hauled himself up in a smooth motion that belied his heavy mass, all feline grace as he landed in a crouch.

Hands that I swore were smoother a moment before ended in extended claws that curved over the rooftop, his knees and thighs bursting with the sort of muscle football players and wrestlers around the world would have turned frog pond green over. But his face was what took on the greatest transformation of all. Those bronzed features, all smooth lined and rounded angles twisted into a grotesque monster until I couldn't reconcile the man with the hideous stone carving stooped over my tomb.

"Dolion?" I whispered, stretching out a hand to touch the gargoyle's face. His mouth hung slightly ajar, and I half expected water to tumble forth. If I hadn't seen his kind overpopulating the rooflines of buildings in the darkest years of Europe's history, I might not have known him for what he was and walked past him in the cemetery just like the community walking groups. But having seen the hideous monsters who stood sentinel over the precious buildings and homes, warding away the worst of that period's evil to keep their homes and families safe...

I stopped hesitating and curved my palm over his ruined cheek. The stone beneath my hand was cool, though for a moment I fancied I could still feel the thrum of his pulse kick beneath the flesh turned cool. No heartbeat emanated from within his hard chest, all the warmth sucked from him, or enclosed within the granite looking mineral that encased his body in this new form.

"I'll see you at sunrise, little sentinel," I whispered, lest I rouse him, though I had little fear of that, truly. He had said he was tired, and I believed him. I had my own jobs to complete tonight, including locate his friend, the vampire, and convincing both him and the bar witch that I wasn't the threat they believed me to be.

And then, with or without my stone friend's help, I needed to create an exit strategy from New Orleans before I ashed someone else by mistake. It seemed there were already rumors that I was some arcane creature of a different sort. I should probably leave before they decide I was a dragon and try to experiment on me, or worse.

That last had been tried before, many times, along with a few other things that didn't turn out so well, for either me or the other parties. It turned out that I survived, even if they didn't. And their paperwork didn't fare so well, either. But in either case, Dolion wouldn't be so excited to find out I'd abandoned my post if I didn't return by the time he awoke.

I pressed up onto my toes until they barely touched the graveyard floor, and still found myself too short to be on eye level with my tame gargoyle. Well, nearly tame. He probably wouldn't want to be called that, but Dolion's preferences weren't tonight's problems.

"I'll be back soon," I promised him, and just because I could, I found the corner of his cold stone lips with mine and left a chaste kiss there that kind of burned with a sensation I hadn't experienced before.

It would be just my luck that I'd be allergic to gargoyle flavored stone.

Ignoring the tingle that wouldn't rub off, I darted away from the stone sentinel clinging to my crypt as I left the safe haven of the graveyard, and the man who trusted me to keep him safe.

The vampire wasn't at the bar the witch ran when I slipped through the doorway. One look at the bar owner who shook her head—either to say the creature I sought wasn't in attendance or that I wasn't welcome in her establishment—told me that tonight wasn't my night. I left as quietly as I arrived, wondering that she didn't have security on the door and then decided that she probably didn't need it after all.

The sting of her viridian gaze lanced through me long after I walked along Bourbon Street alone, letting the crowds pass by me. Each brush of wayward hands or arms reminded me that I remained a part of their civilization, these people, even when I constantly felt apart from each person no matter how I tried to join in with their activities. Strange, that when I finally stopped was when I found the closest acceptance.

Here, amongst the crowd, I could walk freely, be myself. Perhaps I should bring a Dolion along with me next time I decide to socialize by mistake. We could walk along with the crowd, or against the flow and pretend to be who we wanted to be, or just...be.

Perhaps that was the lesson that, after over six thousand years of existence, I had finally managed to learn.

I hoped he wasn't too upset about the kiss I had stolen, if he recalled the pressure of my lips against his stone at all. I had no idea how aware he would be in his grotesque state, though I suspected he chose what to feel and what not to remember at all.

I was in love.

Okay, so I paraphrased. But that was the gist of what he'd said. Not that he was in love *now*... I nibbled on my bottom lip, lost in thought as I walked through the edge of the crowd and out the back of the current party, lost in a darkened space for no more than a handful of breaths before the next on coming crowd engulfed me.

Long enough for an arm to snake out of the darkened space between buildings and tug me sideways into the shadows. Lost in my thoughts of another man, I didn't even put up a fight. Because let's face it. When you possess the ability to flash fry any enemy, fighting isn't really a necessary skill.

Until the day an enemy possesses the skills to avoid said flash frying.

The fact that Dolion still existed bamboozled me. Not that I'd taken a stone lover before, or that he was one. *Yet*. If I had my way, maybe he could be my first.

Maybe.

Or maybe he was a smooth distraction in an otherwise bumpy existence.

I shrugged the uncomfortable admission that, in all my centuries in this world, I had never successfully taken a lover I could commune with intimately without killing the poor man. Or woman, because I tried that once before too. That one hurt. Really hurt.

I hadn't meant to destroy the poor girl, and...

Well. Ash happened.

"You're supposed to scream or put up a fight." The soft voice behind me sounded...amused.

I sighed. "I was busy. And I had other things on my mind. Can we not get this over with? How much to make you go about your night and bother someone else?" I didn't turn around.

All robbers were alike. Tall, or short. They had skin, hair and a beating heart. In a few minutes, when my boy heart ratcheted up a few notches, that m last wouldn't be a problem any more.

Another flash/bang moment brought to the streets of New Orleans by yours truly.

Hopefully the local population would think my display had more to do with fireworks than any supernatural occurrence, thigh with Dolion's friend and the bar witch sniffing about, my chances of surviving unscathed for too much longer grew slimmer by the nightfall.

"The thing is, little firebird, it's you I wanted to find." The amusement dropped from my captor's voice, though his hand didn't.

I sighed again. *Peek-a-boo, I found you.* Or rather, he'd found me. "Sebastian."

"I am indeed."

A snort ripped free from me. "The two of you won't survive here. Your friend looks like he stepped straight from the sixteenth century. You sound like it. The pair of you need to level up, vampire king."

I could *hear* his eyes roll, I swore.

"I can see why he's enamored with you," Sebastian murmured. "But, little firebird, we have a problem with you."

"*You* have a problem with me," I corrected, as another sigh whispered from my lungs. Facing Sebastian for the first time, I stared into the vampire's soulless eyes as he tried to enthrall me and failed. *This is fun. What other tricks would you like to try on me, Mister Vampire?* My patience waned along with my energy as my body began to heat, boding poorly for both myself and my future lover's best friend, plus any other life form in the alley. "Let me set a few things straight. First—"

"She's not a firebird. She's a Firestarter. You should know the difference, Sebastian. And why in the hell are my toes pink?"

CHAPTER SIX

DOLION

Someone had spray painted my toes, claws and all, in the time between when I climbed on top of my Steorra's crypt and when I cracked an eye to check she was sleeping and found she wasn't there. No stranger to graffiti, only in this new form, I'd discovered with Sebastian on an early evening track upon arrival in New Orleans, the night he outfitted me and we found our accommodation. The state of the city's underbelly might have disgusted me had I not seen so many cities in states of deshabille over the centuries, and played warden to them all from my perch above.

Often, I had ignored the plight of the homeless population, protecting only that which was mine under the roofs where I stood sentinel with my brethren until they died out over the years and I traveled with Sebastian to the new world.

Other times, I became involved.

Never had I found the latter course of action to my benefit. Hatred was always the outcome. And after a time, I chose to step away from the people who feared my twisted face and stone colored skin, retreating with my own kind until a girl with pale ringlets captured my heart.

But the woman who stood before me, her heat rising, was not Minette. Ash's bronze hair brushed her shoulders in impossible metallic glints. She looked as far from this world as It was possible to be, the brightness of that hair and those glimmering eyes that darted about my face. Her lips curled as her gaze dropped and she spotted my toes and—

Laughed.

Sweet, and high and contagious.

The corners of my mouth tugged upward. I danced for her, wiggling my bare feet I'd crossed the city on, seeking first her then, when I couldn't find my Steorra, Sebastian. A boon to find both of them together, though in a different circumstance than I would have hoped.

"Please let my fallen star go," I requested my

friend politely. "I don't need to threaten you. While I am immune to her stunning flame, I don't think your kind is."

Sebastian looked at me in alarm that his immortality might be threatened by the slip of a woman he held. "I beg your pardon?"

Ash giggled and batted at his hand. "Let go of me, you old relic. Before I singe you."

The vampire blinked at her, then released her arm, offering me a rueful look. "I understand why you're taken with her."

"Do you?" I tipped my head to one side. "Would you like to tell me how to get the pink paint off, please?"

She glanced down and shrugged. "I mean, it suits you? But I can find you some product to remove it if that's what you need. I have money stashed for food and things."

"Money isn't an issue." Sebastian passed a wad of currency I didn't recognize in my direction.

I glared at him and waved the phone in his direction. "And yet you made me use this."

Tears actually flowed from Ash's eyes. "Oh, this is precious. What are you, five hundred years old? Six?"

I pocketed the phone distastefully and took the

cash Sebastian offered for good measure. "I was born of a stone seed in 1379."

Ash did a quick calculation in her head. "Okay, so five to six hundred years old sans rounding. You?" she directed the same question at Sebastian.

He shrugged. "Give or take."

I knew he expected her to answer in kind, but I wasn't quite so naive. "I'm sure you don't want to spend the night in an alley. Can we go somewhere nicer to clear the air that is less...pressure on you?" I held out a hand, willing myself not to raise it to touch the lips that had grazed mine, the craving to contact the place where she had kissed me too great a temptation to ignore.

My slumber had crept on me almost immediately, heavy and hours overdue. But that light touch of skin on stone ripped through my psyche, tearing me out of my sleep. I strove not to flinch as she laid her lips on mine in the barest contact, then stepped away. But my mouth burned with need and it had taken everything in me not to wrap my hand around her throat and haul her back to me, crush our mouths together and find out what she tasted like with my stone tongue.

A part of me still did crave that twisted need.

I was so lost in the memory, my hours old fantasy, that I nearly missed her answer.

"There's a coffee house a few blocks away. It'll be busy, but it's not stressful. Why don't we have dinner and coffee there and you can...tell me who you think I am and exactly what you think I've done?" She cast a curious glance in Sebastian's direction, then curled her fingers through my hand in the clearest statement she could make.

And I was here for every moment of her sass.

The quaint coffee house Ash picked out was squashed between a nightclub and a mechanic's workshop that Sebastian explained to me. Both businesses looked like they had existed for at least as long as the other in utter disgust of the neighbor that should never have been. One was covered in grease and oil, the other all flowy curtains and spicy scents.

"Turkish?" I murmured, lacing my fingers through Ash's, careful not to hurt her.

Black velvet draped her from neckline to toes, covering her sandaled feet, except for a strip of translucent soft mesh across her middle, baring her stomach and lower back to me. The effect was seductive as she sashayed her way along the street. Standing next to her tiny frame, I became all too aware of how small her body was next to mine. My fingers spread hers wide apart. I closed my hand slowly, giving her the chance to pull away.

My Steorra flexed in my grip then folded her fingers tight against mine. One of those soft sighs I didn't think she knew she made slipped from her lips. "A strange mix of scents and spices and languages, this place," she admitted, leaning slightly into my side as we walked. Sebastian made a huffing sound behind us that I ignored. I would wear his poor humor later. "Creole, French, American...and others. We all exist here together. Accepted," she said, looking down at our joined hands.

Her golden skin wound around my slightly paler version, now that my stone patterns had faded. Her thumb brushed the caved marks on my wrist.

"I was born that way," I murmured, all too aware of Sebastian loitering behind us.

"And your friend?"

My grip flexed around her hand. "He was... created. Not his choice. Or at least, he didn't quite understand the choice at the time. But that's not my story to tell," I murmured.

Ash fell silent as the vampire in question dropped back a dozen paces, his footfalls fading as we approached the small coffee shop. "He has some good manners, doesn't he?"

"On occasion." I held the door for her, and she smiled at me.

"You have some, as well."

"I suspect you come from a time when etiquette was crucial, though a lot older than either of us." I inhaled the scent of her, pure starlight, as she walked beneath my arm.

Ash's eyes fluttered shut as she stood in the doorway of the coffee shop. Her hand untangled from mine and I let her go, still holding the door, bemused. This side of her was something I hadn't seen before as she seemed to absorb the ambience, the heat and warmth and energy of the overcrowded coffee shop.

For just a moment, it was as though the only person in the place was her, the scents tangible as they flowed around her like visible golden threads of spice drawn into her soul.

Then the slipped out of my hand, clanging shut and the moment broke.

"Thanks," Sebastian said dryly, pushing his way inside as I guided Ash toward a table an attendant motioned us toward, menus wielded like a shield against the thrum of conversation that once again filled the small space. Fragments of words bounced from wall to decorated wall, shattering and reforming in an epitome of fragrant white noise.

"I thought crowds bothered you." I settled on a large floor pillow, folding my legs beneath me. Ash curled at my side, apparently perfectly comfortable at ground level. Her black velvet skirt formed a circle around her, though her toes peeked out as she slipped her sandals off and tipped her head back, once again lost in her personal show of bliss.

And took me along with her for the ride.

I trailed my hand down her spine, pleased when she neither flinched nor pushed me away. "What do you recommend?"

"The apple tea. Iced," she replied promptly with her eyes still shut. "And the spiced scones. Though your friend may have other tastes?" I waved a hand to pass her order on to the staff as Ash opened one wary eye, wrinkling her nose when several shawls obscured our vision of the table. "Don't you have a bar to tend?"

The witch stared at her with two wide eyes. "There mustn't be much room in that little cemetery you hide in. And yet you manage to appear well groomed for a grave rat."

Ash offered a one shouldered shrug, much like the woman opposite her, sans the shawls. "I have other— a spare crypt." She caught the slip before she gave her secret away in full, her spine stiffening.

I leaned back, keeping my face carefully blank. When we agreed to head off to the coffee house, Ash disappeared between the graves, leaving me in a brilliant flash only to appear literal moments later, clean and completely changed into the velvet dress she wore now. I held back my suspicions that she kept a house of some sort nearby, but that was her secret to keep.

Sebastian broke the heavy silence that descended over us, his gaze flickering between the two women. "Tifa, Ash. Ash, you know our local witch."

"I know she wants to cage me. Or something." Ash picked up a cinnamon stick encrusted with sugar crystals and nibbled on the end.

"Or something." Tifa held out a bejeweled hand in a peace offering—at least, I thought that's what it was—and raised an eyebrow when Ash didn't move. "Manners," she tutted.

"I have them. You are full of shit," Ash said with clarity.

My laugh boomed around the coffeehouse, halting conversation for a moment before the white noise around us resumed.

I swore my fallen star looked pleased, if only for a fraction of a moment. "I'm glad you're enjoying yourself." I wound the material of her skirt around my fingers, tugging a little. A flush that I was sure had nothing to do with an oncoming crisis stained her skin, though Sebastian sent me a warning look, and I desisted.

Perhaps we can return to this later.

"Tifa, why don't you tell Ste–Ash," I chose my words carefully. "What you think she's done? We can start from there."

Ash studied the witch with the same detached curiosity that spoke of the centuries she well outweighed us in age, I was certain. Sebastian, on the other hand, looked distinctly put out that he wasn't included in the conversation at all.

Tifa shrugged, and her shawls dropped from one shoulder in a practiced move that drew my friend's attention well away from the tempting morsel at my side.

I suppressed a smile of my own, and resumed

tangling my fingers in Ash's skirt. My distraction was short lived, however, with the witch's next words.

"I don't accuse you of anything, and neither should Sebastian. We know who is setting the fires, and setting up your not-phoenix for the fall," she said sweetly, settling into Sebastian's side. He slipped an arm around her waist.

The movement that might have bothered me yesterday didn't hurt my heart half as much as it did tonight.

"Well, don't keep us waiting," Ash muttered, the first bit of impatience entering her tone. "Please let me know who I need to incinerate to be able to live free for this generation?"

"Something about manners." I tapped her leg and found my fingers contacting bare thigh beneath her skirt. Sensation zipped through my hand. Her head snapped to me, and I knew the sharp contact didn't travel in one direction. "Sorry," I murmured.

"You're not." Her hand covered mine.

"We found her. Anitta." Sebastian's good humor dropped, and he pulled Tifa onto his lap.

My head swiveled back toward them and I swore the stone inside my heart cracked right down the middle. "What name did you say?"

"Anitta." Sebastian looked up at me with red

rimmed eyes that told me either he hadn't drank enough, or had too much, though the witch didn't bear the marks on her neck I'd habitually noticed on Sebastian's previous wife. "We didn't end her that night, my friend. She has haunted my dreams for months now."

"And you thought not to wake me? The woman who ended—" My voice rose to a bellow, and only the gentle hand, half the size of mine that covered my knuckles, brought my volume down. "The- the fucking demoness who ended Minette's life still exists?" I hissed.

The scones and tea arrived. I sat back contemplating everything that whirled around my head.

"Who is Anitta?" Ash asked.

I leaned back on my pillow, breathing hard. My mouth opened, and I snapped it shut again, glaring at Sebastian. I hadn't told her in the street, and he could answer her now.

"My sire." The vampire fixed his heavy gaze on Ash, who watched him with a detached sense of curiosity, as though he was a puzzle she needed to solve. "The creature who created me, just as Dolion told you outside." He tapped his ear to indicate his superior skills.

Ash nodded politely. I suspected she had plenty

of her own, and that we needed to constantly not underestimate this woman in all things, but that wouldn't happen while ever we thought we knew more than she did, or our combined egos—and wallets—got in the way.

"Anitta was not a kind mistress," Sebastian said baldly. "She took a mere human, stripped me down to nothing more than a blood crazed demon baby and let me rampage for two hundred years. Then, she tried to train me to be like her."

Ash nodded again. "Did it work?"

Sebastian looked surprised at the question. "Yes. For a time. Then I pushed her away. It was...not a good time in our history. She chased me, and tried to influence my choices. For a time, she existed in my wife's head. Tried to make her harm herself. Killed many we cared about. She is a powerful being, have no doubt. This will be no easy task. We already thought—" Sebastian broke off, staring at me.

Memory washed through my mind of everything we did to try to stop Anitta's dark reign when she returned for him. The demoness and her control over the witch and her wolves that night. Sebastian had been unable to kill the woman who sired him, who created him. My inability to stop the woman I loved from dying. A necklace of blood red beads at her neck as I carried her from the ashes of the burned out house once she ended—once we all thought she ended—Anitta's life.

Once we thought the demoness was dead.

And now she returned, playing with us all this time.

As though waiting for us to lull into a false sense of security. To forget. To fall in love.

To play with us again.

My hand folded around Ash's too tight. Something cracked but she didn't cry out or pull away. I would not lose someone else to that monstrosity again.

This time when the demoness died, it would be to eternal flame.

CHAPTER SEVEN

ASH

The grounds of the Ursuline Convent sat in shadow beneath us in the darkest hours before the false dawn. The moon had long set, and the coffeehouse locked up once we walked away leaving Sebastian and Tifa lost amidst quiet conversation. But Dolion said everything that needed to be said. I had questions, but my answers could wait until he was ready to share what he knew of our future, and the stories of his past.

Instead, I took him to the place where I'd been hiding for the past two years when I wasn't curled in my chosen crypt. At the convent, I chose an unoccupied cell long abandoned for its haunted qualities. The old abbey had a long history of its own to claim, though no nun had inhabited its walls for many years. Only dust collected on shelves wiped down by museum staff at regular intervals now, stealing the heart of what had once been a place of worship, and home to many.

Dolion followed me through my silent tour of the building to the locked third floor where I had lived in secret for the past two years with no knowledge that my cell matched the same room that Sebastian's previous wife had once occupied when she first arrived from France in 1735. The door bore plenty of scars, and the lone cupboard held a handful of dresses I'd been gifted over the ages and kept mostly as keepsakes, memories of lives so they wouldn't be forgotten.

Otherwise, I existed in my regular black tee and yoga pants, having no concept of sweat with my own inner heating issues.

"The halls are quiet. Like..." I didn't finish my sentence, plucking at a dust bunny that clung to my velvet skirt. The ball of lint drifted across the rooftop and over the courtyard before it began its three story descent in slow motion on a night breath.

"Like the grave's silence," Dolion finished. He waved his fingers.

The small motion left the dust motes in a turbulent flight before the lint ball steadied and floated continuously downward and out of sight.

"Sometimes I think they whisper. The nuns who were here before. Like shadows of the past. Stupid, isn't it? Especially when I lived through all of those years. Just... somewhere else," I mused.

"It's not stupid, Steorra. That we lived through those years—you, more than most of us, I believe, does not change that recall the echoes that return from the void of our past, fallen star."

"Why do you call me that?" I whispered, drawing my knees to my chest and wrapping my arms around my legs. I rested my chin on top of everything, viewing the world in shadow, side on. The moon had long set, leaving us in that darkness that suited his words.

"Because you flare bright like the flash of a burning star in its arc across our world," Dolion said simply. "Why do you call yourself after the dullest form of what you become?"

I wave his comment away, still reveling in the fact that he has given me the simplest explanation of what I am, and who I have been that anyone had put into words in nearly six thousand years.

A stone man and a Firestarter.

I snorted into my knees. We sounded like the

perfect match for a barbeque advertisement. "A long time ago, someone called me Shamash. A group of someone's," I murmured, still not looking at him. *Back when fear wasn't the order of the day, and clans worshipped the elements when they didn't understand something they considered greater than themselves.* "It was a bit of a mouthful, so I kept the shortened version. It has nothing to do with what I become."

"You mean they worshiped you as a goddess," Dolion corrected me for my oversight.

I shrugged. "Perhaps. It is better than this running and hiding all the time. Why aren't you scared of me?" *Everyone else is terrified of who I could be. What I might become if I am not caged.*

Smooth fingers traced gently over my hair in a tender massage that began at my temples and worked backward to my nape. "What is there to be scared of, Steorra? The end of this life or this world, the beginning of the next? All things end. I have learned this. I have accepted it. My own mortality has long been a...fixed point." He shrugged, and his touch paused for a breath before his massage resumed again. "But if we sleep and wither away, we forget to live. Then, what does it matter if this world ends on that watch? I would prefer to try again, Steorra. With you."

Those same fingers curved under my jaw, gliding all the way to my chin. Knuckles caught there, lifting gently in a grip I knew he wouldn't let me break, nor did I want to pull away. I allowed him to turn my head, my eyes already shuttering when his breath grazed my lips. Then his mouth settled over mine in a warm, soft touch, so sweet and tender that the tears that broke from beneath my lashes seared my cheeks instantly.

"Dolion—" I whispered, placing a heated hand to his hard chest, a second before my vision whited out, and my world disintegrated in a puff of ash.

I blinked, still curled in the same firm embrace like I had never moved or shifted place at all. "This is unusual," I murmured, running my hands along cool stone arms that didn't budge. Neither did his formidable chest that held no discernable heartbeat that I could fathom. "Uh, how do I get out?"

Ash coated my legs beneath my skirt that held a few burn marks of its own. *Damnit. Not this outfit.* This was why I usually existed in yoga pants and tees. Those, at least, were easy and cheap to replace.

"Do you need to get out?" Amber eyes, lit with some remarkable glow from within, stared down at me.

I nibbled at my lip. "No?"

"Good." Dolion's arms stayed exactly where they were, though this skin warmed as his stone dissipated back to wherever it originated.

The same place where I drew my flame from, I supposed.

A nudge on the top of my head brought my attention back to him. Dolion's eyes locked onto my mouth, and his own quirked as if to say, *Do you wanna try that again?*

Only, of course, he wouldn't use the vernacular, but what the hell. It was fun to imagine the words on him. Then his mouth settled on mine again, and words were the last thing I thought of as his lips pressed against mine, a little more intently this time, and his tongue swept across the seam to push inward.

A soft breath left me in a startled sound. Heat that had little to do with my internal flame and everything to do with the man wrapped around me kindled low in my belly. I mewled against his mouth, parting my lips as his tongue surged inward. Firm fingers resumed their massage against my nape, and the dual sensation overrode every nuance that drove my instinct to self-combust back—well, only in a different way.

The tip of my tongue stroked along his as he

showed me what he wanted, gathering me closer. His heartbeat resumed slow and strong in his chest. I rested my palms over it, needing that rhythm to ground me as his kisses took me to a place I couldn't describe, lost in the headiness that left me floating.

When he finally drew back, my eyes refused to open, the lids too heavy to lift. "Too much, Steorra?"

I shook my head, dizzy with the sensation and leaned into his chest. "No. I've just never—" My brain jammed on the confession, shutting down.

But Dolion didn't call me out on the omission, folding his arms tight around me, blocking out the world for as long as I needed.

And coward that I was, I took the option he offered, resting with my cheek against his chest, reveling in the simple beat of his heart, the warmth of him without fear of incinerating a lover for the first time.

CHAPTER EIGHT

DOLION

I didn't let Ash go home alone. The taste of her incandescence etched deep inside me as I walked beside her, a gift of her trust that, once given, I couldn't release. She didn't utter another word after I kissed her, only led me to the place she seemed to keep most secret from the rest of the world.

Her second gift was letting me walk alongside her in silence as she showed me the way to the secret I guessed she kept away from everyone else. I climbed the twisted staircase behind her that led between an alleyway I discovered that could only be reached from above. Townhouses arched together like so many cards, all ready to topple at a moment's notice. Each wall was painted a different color, the roofs bright, and stained glass patterns decorated nearly every glass surface.

Music played from some of the open windows and more than one person waved as we weaved our way between the colorful abodes. If I had thought that discovering Ash's graveyard hideout or her showing me the convent were signs of her letting me into her life, this blew my mind in all the most incredible ways. I stood at the arched door to her hidden townhouse as she pressed her key to the lock and waited.

Ash spared me a quick glance over her shoulder, a smile softening her features. "Are you coming inside? I didn't bring you all this way to gawk at my neighbors."

I grasped the deep turquoise door that bore plenty of battle scars and that looked like either she or someone else had added a few roses at some point that had faded over time, and waited for her to cross the threshold. "There is so much of you in this place." I gestured to the risen street that glided above everything, and stepped inside her home.

Ash closed the door behind me, not bothering to lock it. I took note of that fact, and slipped my shoes off at the door. She nodded her approval, kicking her own sandals off. "More than you know," she said softly.

A look of hesitation crossed her face before she held out her hand and turned away from me.

I ignored the outstretched hand, and stepped up behind her, sliding my hands around her waist. "I know this is new to you, Steorra. There is no rush."

She laughed, a hollow sound so different from her joy of a moment before. "Isn't there? Don't you think I worry about destroying the people here? Everything that I– that they've built?"

I leaned down, sweeping her hair to one side and trailed my lips across her cheek, over the shell of her ear until she sighed and softened in my arms, though her spine remained taut. "I do, and what you have built here is beautiful. Is this fear of destroying what you have created why you have hidden yourself away for so long? These people love you, Steorra."

She wriggled in my arms. "I like that you call me that way too much."

"There is no such thing, and no need to run anymore." I wrapped my arms around her, testing once to see if she would baulk at the restraint. When she didn't, I tightened my hold, drawing her back against me. "Let me love you, Steorra."

"Dolion," she breathed, heat flooding my arms

the moment her panic hit in full. "I– I don't know how—"

I spun her in my embrace and crushed our mouths together, taking the full brunt of her attack. My tongue slid between her lips without begging permission this time as I cupped the back of her head, lacing my fingers through her silky locks. She moaned in my arms, pressing her breasts to my chest, arching to ease herself closer.

When her tongue traced alongside mine as I thrust into her mouth, tasting the brightness of her from within, the sweet tenderness of her tested every inch of my restraint. Molding my hands to her sensuous body, letting my palms seek out her generous curves and pull her into me, I walked us into the hall she'd been facing when she first held her hand out to me in offering.

Neither of us were under any disillusions of what tonight was. Less than a seduction, more than a joining. We were in unfounded territory, discovering each other with every new step.

"Let me show you," I murmured against her lips, still walking her backwards along the hall.

She tapped the wall when we passed a doorway and I turned her into the darkened room, cradling her carefully to me so I wouldn't bump her against the hard edges.

"My room," she managed, drawing back from me long enough to slide her arms from the dress. The material pooled at her feet and two quick strides brought me thigh to thigh with the naked woman who made my palms ache to hold her.

"You wore no undergarments beneath that flimsy gown?" I growled, biting her bottom lip lightly and not letting go.

A gasp left her. She shook her head, her luminous dark eyes latched onto me. "No," she managed around the way I held her captive.

I nipped her lip gently, earning myself a squeak. The sound zipped straight to my cock that strained against fastenings of my pants. Gliding my hands over her smooth, golden skin, I pulled the heat of her against me, reveling in her bare body pressed to my clothed one.

"Where?" I rasped, barely able to string a full thought together with her so close, so hot pressed to me.

The tip of her tongue flicked playfully against my lips as she found my hand and led me across the darkened room, stopping when my knees hit a tall mattress covered by a silk quilt. Her hand slapped the center of my chest in a decent push. My knees buckled on command. I sat, bemused and aroused as Ash straddled me, resting her hands on my shoulders.

And again, she hesitated, her confidence folding in on herself.

I leaned back on my hands, tilting my head to one side as I appreciated what I could see of the view with eyes that took in so much more than the mortals that overran this world. Her thighs trembled against mine as she let me study her, and her hands squeezed my shoulders rhythmically.

"Undress me," I murmured, giving her hands something to do. The small task should be enough to keep her mind occupied, and her panic art bay. Fine hands fluttered across my shoulders and to my waist. "Start with my shirt," I instructed.

"Thank you," Ash breathed, running her fingers along the row of buttons that held my shirt together, then back up. Starting with the top one, she undid each until my shirt hung open. Her breasts brushed my skin as she pushed the shirt off my shoulders. I helped her with the arms, then her hands dropped to my waist. "How–?"

I ran my hands up her arms, twining my fingers

through her hair and brought her mouth to mine for a deep kiss. "On your knees, Steorra."

A shuddering breath left her as she broke the kiss first and slithered between my legs. Her nails grazed the insides of my thighs through my pants and it took everything I had not to come on the spot. She worked the zipper better than I had, peeling back the loose fitting cotton and working it over my hips. My cock sprang free as she pulled my clothing from my body, leaving me as naked as her. Then her hands returned to scrape the insides of my thighs, traveling upward from my knees, the journey taken in reverse. Hot breath brushed my cock, and her lips grazed my skin.

Breath hissed from my lips. "Come here." I cupped my hands under her armpits, hauling her up to me, but she batted my hands away.

"No. I want to touch you. Please?" Those same lips traced patterns along my inner thigh.

I groaned and tipped my head back, releasing her. "Fuck, Steorra. I have no choice in this, do I?"

"None whatsoever, stone man."

I groaned when her tongue touched my cock, already straightening and rigid when her hand tried to close around my length, and couldn't. Her soft strokes left me tingling all over, and far too close to the edge I needed to avoid. "Like this." I gripped her hand hard, closing her fingers around my cock and worked us together for a few slow pumps.

"Oh," she whispered as I thickened in her grip. "You like that?"

"I like everything you do," I managed through gritted teeth. "But if you keep touching me so softly, I won't make it to sliding inside you, and I very much want to do that with you tonight, Steorra."

"Oh," that same soft breathy sound elicited from her again.

I squeezed out joined hands once more and let go, sliding my hand around the back of her neck. "Come up here?"

But her mouth had different plans, hot and wet as she engulfed my cockhead. Her tongue ran soft, warm circles around my length, just below the crown. I bucked a little into her mouth and she hummed her appreciation, grazing her nails across the hairless skin on my inner thighs.

The hand behind her head tightened. I massaged my fingers into her scalp, giving her time to explore and find her own pace. Ash licked and sucked, pulling her mouth up my length and diving down to choke on me voluntarily.

Blood surged through me, and I pushed up into

her mouth, pushing her head down and holding her there for a second. Her throat constricted around me, and the prettiest sound filled the room as she mewled on my cock. I groaned, pulling her off me and up into my arms.

"Jesu, you're a good girl, Steorra," I whispered, winding her legs around my waist and rubbing her pretty little cunt back and forth across my straining cock already coated with her saliva. "I nearly spilled myself down your gorgeous little throat then." I kissed her softly, offering my apology, but she returned my kisses eagerly, lapping at my tongue with her own until I was close to pushing deep inside her and sheathing myself to the hilt.

But this was her first time and I needed to display greater self-control than I had a moment before, regardless of how much she seemed to have liked my sort of dominance.

Gripping her ass cheeks in both hands, I leaned back and rolled us on the bed so I lay between her spread legs. "Now is the time to tell me you want me to give you an orgasm and stop there, Steorra," I murmured, holding myself above her. I didn't play fair, releasing her rounded ass cheeks to toy with her nipples, rolling the taut peaks back and forth in my fingertips until she writhed for me. The scent of her need filled the room. "We can stop any time."

"You are really fucking mean," she muttered. "Do you know that?"

"Such a filthy mouth," I murmured, licking her lips as she gasped and sighed for me, spreading her legs. "Tell me to stop, Steorra."

"Please," she begged. "I know this will–"

"Hurt?" I kissed the corner of her mouth. "Yes, it will hurt. But with pain can come pleasure. Let me tease you. Let me show you," I whispered, nudging my thick cock against her soaking entrance, never letting up on milking her pretty nipples that loved being played with. "I think you've been ignored for far too long, don't you?"

She shook her head. "I never wanted—"

"Liar," I breathed. I leaned down and sucked the tip of a nipple into my mouth as I pushed the head of my cock into her cunt, just the tip, and worked my hips back and forth. "Fuck, you're wet," I groaned at the noises she made, the soaked slurping sondes as I teased us both with the sensation of wanting to fill her but not quite being inside her.

Ash whimpered and arched beneath me, spreading her legs wider. "Deeper, please," she begged, pushing upward, but I pulled back, teasing her endlessly with the tip of my cock. Edging was my favorite kink, and I'd teach her the madness of needing to come but holding back for days on end, whipping her into a frenzy hour after hour until she was a hot, wet mess who wanted nothing more than to lick and suck and fuck.

"Please," she screamed, as I reached between us and strummed her clit gently.

Heat—not her combustible sort, but the liquid type—gushed forth around my cock as she came for me, weak and trembling. Ash's arms latched around my neck as she sobbed through her orgasm. I held her close and slid all the way inside, her body ready and aching.

Her soft scream as I invaded her body tore at something inside both of us. I held her all the tighter, waiting until the trembling in her legs lessened, the cries against my chest turned to softer breaths.

"I'm going to move, Steorra," I murmured to her temple, laying kisses against her skin as I thrust my hips deep. "Let me show you—"

It didn't take more than another thrust before her cries turned from pain to pleasure, her nails digging into my shoulder blades.

"Are you alright?" I murmured, "I can stop."

"Don't you dare, stone man," she panted beneath me, locking her heels behind my waist. "If you don't keep going, I'll find a toy and finish myself off while you watch."

My cock swelled at the thought of watching her play with herself. *A game to play on another night.* "Tempting, but right now you have a different toy to play with." I slammed deep, filling her until my hips met hers, and groaned at the way her searing walls strangled my cock. "Hells, Steorra. I'll be addicted to having you wrapped around me."

Another thrust, two and she clamped down on me hard. Ash pulled my mouth to hers, kissing me desperately as she flooded my cock with her juices. Her cunt milked me as I had her nipples minutes before. I growled my release to the darkened room, slamming deep as I came, locked inside her.

Our bodies rocked gently through the rest of the night, working out variations of pleasure and pain as she screamed softly for me again and again. I filled my fallen star with my seed, claiming her as my own and knew my heart would never be as empty or as shattered as it had been these last three hundred years again.

CHAPTER NINE

ASH

I woke in the arms of a stone man. A literal stone man, without a heartbeat.

I slapped Dolion's chest and earned myself a stinging hand for my troubles. "This is not comfortable," I told the dead man beneath me," and swore I heard a rumble within his solid chest in reply.

Between my legs ached, though not in a bad way. My thighs throbbed, and the scent of him, all spice and musk of an age gone long by was all over me. I didn't object to any of it. Finally—freaking *finally*—I managed a lover who didn't combust on impact. Or thrust, in my case.

Not only was Dolion apparently fireproofed, or fire repellent in any case, he also had a way of bringing me back from the edge of my worst panic attacks. The moment one came on last night, he kissed me and provided the perfect distraction from what made taking a lover so terrifying.

Instead of igniting the world, he only created a long, hot burn inside of me—and maybe, him. That, I didn't object to at all. And so I cuddled my stone stature of a man, twisted gargoyle features and pink toe nails and all, and fell back to sleep.

The sun had set when I woke to a frantic knocking on my door. I sat up next to a human looking Dolion rather than the gargoyle stone version, and rubbed my eyes. "It's open," I called groggily, wondering which of my neighbors had run through their weekly groceries or had enough juicy gossip that they simply had to share the good news right *now.*

Except it wasn't a neighbor who strode through my house and right into my room. It was a vampire.

"Did I really just invite you in? Get out." I flapped at Sebastian's silhouette. "The two of you are turning me into a bat."

He frowned. Okay, my eyes were closed and I

couldn't see it but I could feel him frowning. "You don't look like a bat."

"No, but now I have the nocturnal habits of one."

"And you have strange sleeping arrangements. Didn't you slap me last night?"

"I found a stone man with no heart beat in my bed," I reminded Dolion as he sat up, apparently completely refreshed and right as rain.

"Stop it," Sebastian snapped. "I didn't come here to find you playing lovers with each other."

"I thought that was the point you were trying to make when you dragged me out of my sleep," Dolion said in a pointed voice.

I didn't think he meant the few hours we managed wrapped in each other's arms.

A feral sound escaped the vampire that might have been stuck somewhere between a snarl and a growl. "Anitta. I found her. And she's impersonating your firebird." Sebastian whirled and left my home in a flurry of mutters and suppressed curses even as Dolion's fingers stiffened on my spine.

"I suppose our brief honeymoon period is over then," I said ruefully, stretching along his body, and rested my fingers on his muscular stomach. How *much* muscle this man possessed blew my mind. Just like how much of...other things his body had.

Dolion didn't move for a long moment. So long that I thought he might have reverted to his other state.

"You should stay here," he said finally, slipping out of my bed and grabbed his clothes without looking at me.

"What?" I lay in the bed alone, half covered by the sheet I'd pulled up out of habit, though my body heat didn't really require it. "No. I'm coming with you."

"Steorra." Dolion, already half dressed, finished buttoning his pants. He crouched before me, and clasped both hands around my face, staring into my eyes. "The last time I faced this enemy, she took from me everything my heart desired." His voice rasped on that last word and though no tears swap across his gaze, the pain that darkened his amber eyes was undeniable. "I wouldn't repeat that occasion. Not with someone that I—"

He broke off, and placed his mouth over mine in a gentle kiss that might have lasted a breath or an eon. I couldn't tell which before he was gone and the door to my home swung gently shut behind him while I was still recovering.

But I had my own means of transportation, and

Dolion wasn't the only talented one around here who liked to get his own way with a kiss.

Even if it was a good kiss. A really damn good kiss.

My lips tingled as I pulled on a bright orange dress, hand embroidered with gold and turquoise threads. Two of my favorite colors. One of my neighbors had embellished the gift for me years ago and I'd loved it so much the material had softened with wear. That didn't prevent me from flashing my way to the highest point I knew—the convent—and then across the city d to the place where cross gathered in a fury.

Because that was where I would find her, the woman pretending to be me.

And she did a decent job. Kind of.

Anitta, terrifying demoness and sorcerer supreme—it sounded like yet another rip off superhero movie in the making—stood on top of my crypt in my graveyard, wielding flame from both hands.

I never did that, but it's kind of impressive. Waste of energy though.

Her laugh cackled madly across the graves. If she was going for an effect of madness and disrespect in front of the city's populace in my name, she'd certainly achieved it from the disgruntled mutters that surrounded me. Hate brewed faster than love and I'd spent the last years hidden away, my true nature a secret I kept to myself and more recently, one other.

Only those in my treetop street knew something about me was different, even if they didn't know *what* exactly. I kept that part of myself secreted away, too.

Friendless. Alone.

The years and decades of accumulated nothingness filled the expanding void inside me as my own heat built, the panic overwhelming as always. *Dolion, I need your kisses now.* But his attention was locked right where it needed to be: on the threat of the woman who was far more dangerous than I gave credit for initially. Fake as fuck she might be, but this creature wielded my flames in a PR campaign I couldn't match.

She had planned this night well and I didn't know how to fight, except with my own fire. And that, for this city, just like all others through my turbulent history, would be catastrophic.

"The hair is a bit off," I said from my place right behind Dolion and Sebastian, managing to scare the shit out of both from the way the vampire and the gargoyle jerked.

Sebastian barely spared me a glance, his attention returning to his sire as Dolion spun about to face me, his expression twisted into his stone grotesque form for a moment, fury reflected in his citrine eyes. "I told you to—"

"You don't tell me to do anything," I said flatly. "We aren't there yet, stone man."

His mouth thinned into a tight line before thick arms engulfed me. "You scared me."

"I know," I said, proud, though my words came out muffled against his chest. "I'm claiming it."

He laughed into my hair, crushing me against his impossibly huge body. "You shouldn't be here. It's not safe for you."

Large hands petted my hair, sliding through the tangled mass I hadn't bothered to brush before I zipped across town to find out what all the fuss was about. Light flashed about us as the demoness continued her stage show.

"Nowhere is safe for me. But also, don't leave me like that. It was rude."

"You're right." His words stopped me when I struggled against his chest and I looked up at him to find him staring straight down at me and ignoring the world and all that went on around us. The crowd, the mad cackling creature. Everything. He focused solely on us. "I was scared. Scared that I would lose the woman I loved the second time. To the same creature. Because of the same evil."

My breath stalled. "That's not going to happen," I managed, squeezing my thighs together where the evidence of our midnight fantasies still dampened my skin. "And you're just saying that because you have to, because you took my virginity last night, and I mean, who helps out a six thousand year old creature who couldn't get herself laid in six freaking *millennia*—"

Dolion's mouth crushed mine in a kiss to end all kisses. The crowd's muttering and hate disappeared as the scent of him enveloped me, midnight promises and eternity and peace in that touch. I sighed in his arms, letting go of everything that panicked me, letting him in. Letting him hold me.

"I love you, ma Steorra," he whispered against my lips. "Not because of some outdated version of chivalry, or because you think I owe it to you. Because you are everything to me, and I will not live in this world with a beating heart without you."

I smiled against his mouth. "What more can a girl want?"

"Eternity together."

"Not going to happen if that bitch gets her hands

on your woman." Tifa materialized beside us in a flurry of shawls. She flapped her tassels at me. "You should not be here."

I sighed in the circle of Dolion's arms. "Why does everyone keep saying that?"

"You don't know how powerful she is." Sebastian backed into Dolion as a wave of heat blasted over our heads. Everyone else ducked. Dolion didn't move as Sebastian cursed, tucking Tifa into his arms. "We should not be here."

"And yet here we are. Should we not just get this showdown over and done with?" I waved a hand in Anitta's direction, and frowned at the vampire. "Is there a rule about not killing the one who made you, or something?"

Sebastian's gaze locked onto me. "Not for lack of trying," he grated. "She might look ridiculous up there, but don't be fooled. This woman can turn a crowd against you in seconds."

Dolion's hands closed on my arms. "You shouldn't be here, Steorra," he rumbled, the sound merging with something deeper inside him.

I glanced up at his face, frowning. "Alright, then we take this showdown on the road, to somewhere quieter, you all move away and, *poof*, ash. Simple. Okay?" I said brightly.

The vampire and the gargoyle sighed.

"Steorra..."

"Alright, what am I missing?" I searched their faces. "*Tell me.*"

Dolion tightened his hold on me. "We're leaving."

I looked up at him, placed my hand on his chest. His heart pounded strong, but fast. *Fear.* I could almost scent it rolling off him.

"Alright. We will fight her another day."

Breath left him in a long *whoosh*. "Thank you, my star." His lips brushed my temple and something around my ribs popped as he crushed me to him in a hard hug, moving us through the back of the crowd in long strides.

A fireball whisked over our heads, halting our path.

"That one had a really good aim," I muttered, peeking around his shoulder, and paid proper attention to the demoness for the first time.

"Too good," Dolion agreed, and sighed. "I guess we are doing this your way, Steorra."

Another fireball zoomed over my head, close enough to singe hair. *Ugh, I hate that smell.*

"I guess so."

I turned to face my foe, the woman who had

dressed like me, and wore a facsimile of my face with terrible hair. The only difference was that hers wasn't on fire.

And she stood less than five paces away, wearing a terrible, terrible smile on her face as she sank her blade deep into Sebastian's side.

And the vampire dropped to the trampled grave dirt beneath our feet.

CHAPTER TEN

DOLION

The world flashed around us once, then again. Long enough for the bar to come into view, blood that wasn't mine to splatter my hands mixed with a fine coating of ash, for Tifa and Ash to shout at each other, and the world to disappear again.

I stood in a darkened hall, breathing in dust and stale air outside a locked door while my fallen star ranted and raved on the other side in a tiny room. Sebastian would heal on his own. She'd checked on him briefly, made sure he wouldn't die, before she ran. And hid away from the world for failing him, and herself.

Tifa was scared. Just as I had been at the grave-yard, but that didn't mean any of us blamed Ash for what had happened. That was on the demoness alone and maybe us for turning our backs on her when we knew better.

And now we wore the scars of her wrath. Or at least, one of us did.

"Steorra." I knocked softly after a minute. "Please let me in."

The ranting stopped. "You said she was a risk to *me*. Not to him."

"She was always a risk to all of us. To everyone." I rested my knuckles against her door. "Please, will you unlock this?"

She fell silent. A flash beneath the doorway and a smattering of ash across my bare toes—still pink, though some of the paint had begun to wear away—and she arrived next to me. Her sunset orange dress hung in tatters. The edges were singed, the center smeared in blood and sins that didn't belong to her.

I held out my arms and she fell into my embrace, sobbing. "I am sorry I didn't protect you better," I whispered, taking her to the ground with me, where she curled into my lap, trembling and shaking.

Heat seared me, her tears boiling my skin. It was warning enough to bring on my change. My skin hardened to my stone form a second before the world whitened out again. I sank back into the darkness that I'd remained in for so long, taking refuge in my stone state, not knowing if she stayed with me or not, letting my Steorra burn herself out against my gargoyle form.

I retained my stone form for far longer than I would have normally, unsure how long she would need, but when I returned to her, my fallen star shivered in my cold embrace, her body coated in ash that smeared her all over. Around us, in a shattered radius, the third floor of the convent bore burn marks in a circle that rippled right across the hallway and up the walls.

Time didn't pass the same way for me in my tone form as it did for her. I didn't know how long she had burned for, alone, but I held her as she shivered and shook and cried, until she finally opened her eyes and stared up at me, all of her heart break right there to see.

"He could have died, and I could have saved him. All because I. Was. Fucking. Flirting. With. You." A great sob tore through her throat. She coughed into her hands, bending at the waist with the force of her grief.

I caught her chin, winding my body around hers. "But he is immortal, ma Steorra, and he did not die. No blade of the demoness' can end his life." Other things might, but not that. Not so simple. Anitta liked to play with her toys before she ruined them, but Ash didn't need to know that right now.

"I should have fried her. Like I said." More sniffles arose as I stroked her hair and sighed.

"And hurt everyone in the vicinity in the process. Which is why you did not flash fry the bitch." I waited.

Her lips twitched against my chest. "Did you—" She cleared her throat. "Did you just use modern slang?"

"I did. Do not expect to hear it again any time soon, Steorra." I laughed softly. "Now, may I clean you, please? You are... dusty." I patted her rump. A puff of ash filled the air.

"That was all you, stone man, not me." Her muffled laughter came from the realm of my armpit.

"If you say so, Steorra. Are there washrooms in this place?"

She let me carry her into the staff bathroom along the hallway, leaving her scorch mark well behind.

"I hope the staff don't come up here ever again. They already think this hallway is haunted as all hell," she muttered, rubbing her cheek against my chest.

"I'm sure with your flashing lights and flame and smoke and ash, there is little chance you haven't assisted the mouth at some point. Steorra," I murmured, placing her under the old faucet and turning on the water. "Is this how it works?"

Jets of rusty water poured over her body as she shrieked like a banshee. "Fuck, that's cold! Off! Off!" Ash clawed at me, pulling herself out of the russet colored puddle that mixed with the soot covering her body. The colors melded in a red and black spiral as she pulled her ruined dress off her body and tossed it away.

"Ahh—" I stared at the other faucet. "This one?"

Ash grumped at me curtly. Water streamed down her face, her hair hanging in damp strands across her cheeks. "Step away from the shower, Dolion. Your rights have been revoked. Wait. Have you not been showering since you arrived? Filthy gargoyle," she berated me under her breath.

"Sebastian has a spa tub with a mix tap," I offered helpfully.

"A *mixer* tap," she corrected me.

"Yes. One of those." I nodded, smiling. "It's much easier." I mimed pulling the single silver bar outward and quoted the vampire who more than likely had not healed by now and quoted him, complete with the little finger actions he favored. "'Set and forget'."

"Ha. He's got you trained, alright." She flurried around the taps, adjusting the water temperature to her liking and tipped her head back, reveling in the fine spray that cleared of rust after a few minutes. "Better. " She held out her hand without opening her eyes. "Join me?"

"Am I permitted after my faux pas?" I touched the tips of my fingers to her own, pleased when she curled her hand in mine.

"You are permitted, gargoyle."

I stripped, tossing my clothes across the room and stepped into the tiled section behind her, sliding my hands along her lower back. "I wasn't sure if I had to beg for your forgiveness after making you so wet."

A giggle erupted from her, the sound shattering the peace in the steam fogged room. "I thought you promised not to dip into the vernacular, you filthy, filthy gargoyle."

"You have no idea how filthy." I cupped her breasts, squeezing her nipples.

"But I just got clean." Ash moaned softly, arching for me. Her head tipped backward, resting on my shoulder. Pert buttocks pressed against my stomach.

I dropped one hand to grip her hip, holding her tight against me. "Do you want me to fix that, Steorra?" I leaned down, sucking the tip of her ear into my mouth and flicked the shell with my tongue.

She gasped, pulling away as I pinched her nipples and pushed her forward into the wall tiles coated with spray. "Fuck, cold—"

"You'll manage," I growled in her ear, tapping her feet apart. Her soft mewl told me she wouldn't fight me any further, and I rolled her nipple between my fingers as a reward until she writhed for me.

Her hands slipped between us, reaching for me, but I batted her touch away, unwilling to spill myself so quickly this time. "But Dolion—" she objected, straining for me. Her nails scratched my stomach.

I gripped her wrists, pinning them at her lower back. "No, fallen star. You'll do this my way tonight." Another nipple pinch reminded her what she liked, and she nodded quickly. "Hands on the wall." Her hands went up with the sort of speed that drew a deep laugh from my chest as warm water rained over us. "Very good, Steorra. Head back, now."

I leaned down and licked her lips leisurely as I reached one hand between her legs, gathering some of her slick to coat her nub and swirling it there, over and over while she whimpered for me. My tongue touched hers lightly, but I denied her both her orgasm and my kiss, leaving her dripping and aching as long as possible, still milking that nipple between my fingers until she rubbed herself between my hand and the wall, frantic and desperate to come.

"Fuck, you're so beautiful like this," I whispered, trailing my tongue across her bottom lip. Saliva dripped from the tip into her mouth. "Swallow for me."

She did on reflex, her tongue peeking out to swipe the last of the fluid for her lips before she realized what she'd done. Her eyes flared wide as I tapped lightly at her clit. Once, then again and pressed down.

She came for me, sweetly, the shower filling with the scent of her satisfaction. I notched at her entrance and surged inside her, thick and veined and hard as fuck to fill her soaked cunt with my seed.

Ash screamed for me, long and hard as I seated myself deep. Her walls closed tight on my cock, strangling my length in her searing heat. "Fuck, fuck, fuck," she chanted, clawing at the tiles.

I released her nipple, closing my hands around hers on the wall. "Keep screaming for me," I growled, drawing back and ramming deep into her heat. Despite my desire to fuck her until the sun rose over the convent, I wasn't going to last half as long as I wanted at this rate. She felt too good wrapped around me. "Christ, Steorra. Your body was made to fit mine."

Her cries and whimpers filled the room, shattering and reforming as I thrust into her over and over again. Even as the water ran cold, her body heated with her orgasm. I pulsed against her, slamming my hands into the wall. Tiles cracked above her head as stone replaced skin over my body a fraction of a breath before she exploded. Even in my stone state I felt the echo of her through the void of darkness that separated my gargoyle state from life.

I opened my eyes to find her writhing on my steaming stone form, still in the throes of her orgasm, impaled on my granite cock, thick and heavy and unyielding inside her. A roar ripped deep from within my soul as I came, filling her with my seed, marking her as mine and no others.

"Ma Steorra," I whispered. "Forever."

She shivered for me as I clasped her body against mine, and rubbed her cheek to the back of my hand like a kitten. "*Notre amour brûlera pour toujours.*"

My breath stopped as though my change had

been forced as her words rippled around my head in my own language.

I stared at the shattered bathroom tiles, the ash that floated in the air surrounding us, speckling the once white walls. The scorch marks that matched the one in the hall.

Our love will burn forever.

My Steorra didn't need to say *I love you*. Her words meant so much more.

Once before I thought I had died at the hands of a demoness when she stole love from me once before, and though I loved then, I thought it had been my once in an existence's chance.

I was wrong.

My lips melded to Ash's as I kissed her deeply, putting everything I couldn't say into her the tenderest touch I could. Nothing could take her from me. Not Anitta. Not time. Not the riled mob the demoness drove to madness with the lies she whispered into their minds.

I had to protect this woman at every cost.

CHAPTER ELEVEN

ASH

I knew what Dolion sacrificed in order to defeat Sebastian's maker the first time, and the cost to them all. Three hundred years encased in stone was not my idea of a good time, nor from the way he spoke—rarely—about those days, was it his. I might only have known the gargoyle for a few short days but in my existence, time meant little compared to the connection we had carved out with each other.

Media made out that an immortal weighed years in the blink of an eye, discarding time as though passing eons meant little to the heart to the individual, when in truth, the reverse held over every one of us.

Each second cost us painful breaths, ruminating

on each failure, every moment relived over and over until we were like to drive ourselves mad. That was the true weight of an immortal life—not the freedom mere humans projected upon themselves, viewing the epochs passing as some sort of glorious frolic through the ages.

What humanity failed to take into account was the culmination of a lifetime—multiple lifetimes—of eros bounding one upon the other, building and building until the frustration and anxiety of every single flaw and frailty and imperfection culminated in a chaotic sense of madness.

Perhaps that was where my flame originated. I didn't recall a time when my panic didn't bring on my heat, obliterating everything around me. Every one.

Until now.

Dolion alone withstood my fury, my fear. And for that, he deserved everything I could give to both him and his friend. No matter that I didn't particularly like the vampire on sight, for no other reason than he annoyed me at a base level. I didn't know, perhaps he reminded me of someone I'd met before, long ago.

Dolion slept over my bed, muscular thighs

crouched low. Pink toes peeped over my heavy wooden bedhead, able to withstand the weight of his statuesque form. His twisted, horrific features no longer unnerved me, but offered a different sort of comfort, knowing who lay inside that stone monster as I rested.

But as before, when he awoke, I wouldn't be there, because I had work to do. And he would just have to forgive me for my sin.

I placed a gentle kiss to the corner of his lips, nuzzling my cheek to his. "We burn together, forever," I whispered, knowing he couldn't hear me. "Wherever we are."

Because I wasn't certain, after what he'd told me about the story of Minette and Sebastian and Gisella and the masquerade party at their original home, that I would be able to deal with the demoness in the way I hoped. But I would give it my best, and hoped that washing around her in the most magnificent way possible, would be enough.

Just enough. That's all I needed it to be. To keep Dolion safe.

Because he was right. Existence and mortality meant little, if those we cared for were threatened. He had come to that conclusion well before me, I knew. He fell first. But I was his fallen star, still burning brightly. My fall was still in progress, and I knew exactly where I wanted my end to be.

I walked out of my home, leaving my gargoyle above my bed with the knowledge that I may never come back.

But everyone in my life, after this, should be safe.

Or so I prayed, though to whom, I wasn't sure. The other gods never spoke to me, after all.

I perched on the top of my crispfied crypt, swinging my legs and drinking a Hurricane from a plastic glass with a matching, lurid green straw that was almost as long as the cup itself. I'd flashed about the city enough where Anitta had been putting on her little stage shows pretending to be me, keeping my distance but in view just enough to gain her attention. Here, then gone. There then away.

Like the flea on the dog's back that couldn't be scratched. Then I settled in on my burnt out crypt, and I waited.

Spoilers: I didn't have to wait long.

The demoness had the attention span of a gnat.

"Aren't you just the flashy one?" Anitta waltzed around my crypt as I sipped my drink.

One, hurricanes, two hurricanes, three hurricanes, too much rum in my veins...

"Says she who ruined my last three pairs of yoga pants."

I tipped the last of my plastic glass—best oxymoron ever—back and managed not to choke. Tifa had made the drink for me under duress but cut back on the alcohol, thankfully. I'd gone off rum back sometime in the seventeen hundreds during my pirate phase and still couldn't talk about it. But Tifa assured me this was New Orlean's super power and I'd better get used to it, if I intended to stay. I rattled the lime colored plastic at my lover's enemy and slung the plastic strap around my neck for safe keeping. It would all be ash in a moment, anyway.

Anitta wrinkled her nose. "I guess there's no accounting for dress sense, really. I can't abide by pants. Or your choice of hair color. Don't your things stink of death? Though that's a cause I could get behind. How does your ass fit in that small space?" She peered at me and wiggled her hips.

My face fell away to be replaced by the creature beneath. All peeling skin, and yellowed eyes stared out at me, more hideous than the creature Dolion had described Sebastian to be when he first turned from human to vampire under this woman—no, this demoness, I corrected myself mental—under her watch. And now, I got to see who she really was..

Disgust roiled within me at the bones that protruded through the fine layers that couldn't really be called epidermis. Hair hung in clumps. I could bet that she didn't tug on too hard in case it fell away and couldn't be reattached. And the smell—oh, the smell.

"I think I prefer the crypt, actually," I said softly, trying not to inhale too hard. "Is this what happens when an immortal dies and can't leave this world? I pity you. And also, your hair." I waved to the misshapen clumps lumped atop her hair that looked like they had once been stunning locks, possibly silky, but not for many hundreds of years. "You really can't go anywhere else, can you? Is it by choice," I continued out of pure curiosity, "or is it because you can't stand the thought of not existing anymore?"

I stopped short of asking how old she was. After all, who really cared? At the end of the long day, when the universe no longer turned on, we were all old. Ancient and should have been frittered away by the least breath left in the cold night air. But for whatever reason we continued while others died. A freak miracle at best, and a tragedy, at worst.

Anitta's rotting lips pulled back to reveal teeth

the same yellowish hue as her stained eyeballs. "Do not pity me, you pathetic small firebird. You think you are bright and fantastic but his love will fade as all things do." Her snarl broke off in a hiss that sounded like a broken tube letting out air from a puncture.

I rolled my lips inward. "Do you have that much magic left?" I asked quietly. "Or have you used it up on your tricks and shows? I know you used to be very powerful."

She will run in spite of herself. Do not be fooled by appearances or any line she feeds you.

Tifa's words drifted across my mind. I kept my distance, remembering the stories, what this demoness had done to Sebastian's wife. But that was before and now...

"I am more than you will ever be, small creature," Anitta declared. "I have slain my firstborn. He, who was ended by my hand, gives me strength. I will rise stronger than ever at the birth of the new day," she proclaimed, her hideous cackle less of a war cry and more an off key screech.

I still didn't move from my perch on my crypt, though I did throw a thumb over my shoulder. "Your first born? You mean that one?" I gestured to Sebastian where I knew he and

Tifa entered the graveyard. Most likely with Dolion, but I'd deal with the pink toed gargoyle later.

After.

If.

"You aren't supposed to be alive." Anitta stared over my shoulder, and squinted.

I waited for one of her eyes to pop from her skeletal face and plop onto the grave below her feet in a jelly puddle and was so disappointed when it didn't happen.

"Neither are you, maman," Sebastian said softly from somewhere at my back. He didn't seem to want to bring Tifa closer, and nor did I blame him. The horror that stood before me was bad enough.

"And I thought we were doing everything together. Forever, Steorra," Dolion's growl grew louder.

I tested where I perched, waving a hand out, but it was too late. He swept forward and the knife that had pierced Sebastian's side pricked my throat. The tang of blood—not mine, not yet—stung my nostrils.

A derisive laugh burst from me. "Didn't you even clean the blade, you hag?"

"You, *dare*," she shrieked, digging the point into

my throat. This time fresh blood flowed, warm and thick from my throat.

Dolion's mouth opened in horror, but I smiled.

"*Forever. Remember?*" I mouthed the words that wouldn't have been heard anyway beneath the mad woman's cackle that filled the graveyard. I wondered if she didn't try to resurrect every soul in it. Then we would have a different battle on our hands.

"I remember." His voice barely made it to me over the white noise floating around me as heat built deep within my core. "I remember everything about you, Steorra."

A storm brewed deep within me as I stood still, letting the flame burning constantly within my soul wash over me for the first time in my life without panic. Without fear. My eyes shuttered as I breathed in my last, savoring the freedom of my lungs expanding on the warm night air.

Feet shuffled as Dolion herded Sebastian and Tifa back out of range. I hoped he would move them far enough. Tears that weren't for me tracked my cheeks, turning to steam on contact.

Anitta's hands curled around me, pulling me back into her body. I let her touch me, let her draw me close to her heart, her fragile, rotting skin. Let her saliva dribble onto my bare shoulder where my cheesecloth shift, the simplest piece I owned, soaked through immediately.

From dust we came, and to ash we shall return.

I opened my eyes, seeking only Dolion out. He stood much closer than I wanted him to be, his muscular legs spread in a defiant stance. Tifa and Sebastian huddled at the far end of the graveyard, almost out of sight, where they needed to be. Good. That was good. They were safe.

Dolion, however...

"We will have words," I told him, my tone hitching as the blade pressed into my skin.

"You have nothing," Anitta told me.

"You will die, I murmured back, all show and pomp gone from me, my energy depleted except for one last act. I had no time left for anyone, except for my stone man who stood opposite my crypt, who refused to move no matter the consequences.

"Forever, Steorra. You promised me." Amber eyes glinted with the fire that would soon reign.

I nodded, and let out my breath. Released my flame. Let it build. Heat wavered the air around me even as Anitta cackled again. Madder and stranger than ever.

"You can't kill me," she gloated, her blade cutting into the soft skin at my throat. Fetid breath of the not so recently dead wafted over me in a sickening sweet-and-evil mixture that would have sent any lesser being to their grave instantly, but I was no stranger to death. "I have been around since the dawn of time."

Dolion smiled at me, the faintest reflection, a mirror image of that same smile he gave me the first time he waited outside my crypt in the graveyard. Not so long ago but an age all the same. He didn't shift or move or run or cower, not with all his muscle, or his inner strength that gave the same to me. Peace passed over my body as I breathed in, remembering the way he held me in the convent, how he sat with me on the rooftop the first time he took me there. The way he showered me in cold water, and the first time I showed him my true home. All the parts of me that he understood, and that I learned about him. Because while I was so busy showing him everything about me, what I'd learned about him was that he had nothing. No home, no place. No one.

Just the people in this graveyard.

The mad impostor who sired his best friend and murdered his lover three hundred years ago. The best friend who woke him because he couldn't stand to be alone with the grief he hid and longer. The witch who tried to love an immortal she wasn't sure could love her back, and...

Me.

I matched Dolion's soft smile and turned in Anitta's coiled embrace. The wiry thinness of her resurrected arms strained as I twisted all too easily in her grip. She gaped at me as I let her blade slice my neck, the burn from my insides already roiling through me, the pain from her deep cut familiar as an old friend.

A sharp inhale told me Dolion took his last breath as I expelled the life force inside of me.

"You made a mistake, demoness. I am no firebird." I stared into her eyes, speaking while I still had the ability, my voice fading with every word. "I am the Dawn," I whispered, as the tip of her knife nicked something important, and blood flowed forth in a river that would end my life. "And my friend is Time. You cannot outlive what birthed you, creature."

Anitta stared in bewilderment at me. Her face, after all she had suffered as she strove for greater power, was almost comical, but I had no life left. No blood. No breath.

Just fire.

Light and heat burst from me and obliterated

everything within my radius. What remained of her pitiful, rotted flesh curled as it peeled away from sharp bone already protruding through frail flesh. Her eyeballs boiled in their sockets as the demoness danced macabrely in her own juices. Bones creaked in their joints, cracked and shattered until in the end all that was left were twin piles of ash that a warm wind brushed away watched over by a silent stone sentinel.

And I died again.

CHAPTER TWELVE

DOLION

My world remained dark no matter how much I struggled to fight against my stone state.

She's not gone. She's not gone.

But my heart refused to believe anything but. The ache in my chest swallowed the grief that lay beneath the pain, though I knew it was there anyway. I'd seen the demoness cut her throat, watched my Steorra's body fall as both life force and flame erupted from her, taking the world along with it.

And I retreated inside myself, taking my stone form as my heart stopped beating and refused to start once again.

My fallen star is gone.

And coward that I was, I couldn't make myself look to check for the pile of ash that would be swept away and face the rotting pile of flesh that Sebastian would have to fight alone, if he hadn't already run from his maker.

The ruined creature that ended Ash's life.

Hot tears tracked my cheeks, only they didn't belong to me. Because stone men didn't cry.

Something told me that Ash would have an inappropriate comment for that, but I didn't wait for another minute without her passing to find out. My eyes flung open before my arms reverted to their moveable state. I searched the graveyard for her and came up...

Empty.

Absolutely empty.

Every row was devoid of people, from what I could see from my immovable position in the center of the graveyard where I had placed myself between the demoness and the tiny fragment of family that is still claimed as some sort of home.

And inside the radius of the devastation the woman I loved would create when she died.

Tears that were mine joined the cooling ones already decorating my cheeks.

"Steorra," I croaked, staring at the blackened

ground that covered every available surface. Every single marble crypt, grave or stone was stained jet black, and ash embers, some still alight and glowing red or amber at the edges. "I am sorry."

"I am not." Soft, warm lips grazed the corner of mine in an undeniable touch that left me aching in a different way.

My skin warmed with her gentle breath on my cheek and the tears blurring my vision of her stunning face doubled. "You returned."

"I did."

"I thought you were dead."

"I was." Her arms embraced me as I folded over her, my stone retreating before I stiffed.

"Steorra. The demoness. Is she—" I wrapped an arm tight around her back, twisting about but the graveyard stood as empty as it had before.

"I do not know." Ash pressed her body to mine, and for the first time, I detected the faintest tremor running through her body.

A shiver, not unlike the one from when she sobbed herself into a mess in my arms on the floor of the convent that night, covered in ash, rippled over her.

I crushed her against my body. "You're exhausted. What do you remember?"

"I remember—" She stalled, and dark eyes rose to meet mine. "Dolion, I remember dying."

I kissed her hard. "I left you. I was scared I'd wake and you would be gone," I rasped against her mouth, drinking in the warmth of her, the way she softened beneath my touch and let me be rougher with her. "I was a coward."

"Because you thought I was gone and you lost love again?" She shook her head. "No, Dolion. You grieved. That is not cowardice. But I am here. And she is..." She shrugged. "I suppose she's gone. I did not see anything beyond my own death. The blackness. The heat. The cold. After."

I swallowed and squeezed her tight. Too tight. "The void, and the echoes of life within."

She nodded against my chest. "Yes."

I'd never told anyone what I heard within the stone. The whispers she spoke of that night, admitted to hearing the dead talk to her in the quiet hours, the nuns of the past talking to her through the void in the moments when she merged with the places between...that was what I also experienced in my stone state.

Sometimes, I hoped to hear Minette, but she had never spoken to me. I never could identify the voices, only knew that the whispers were there and that the more I tried to listen, the harder the conversations were to hear. And so they remained simply echoes within the void, the spaces between life and death where I existed in my stone state.

"I love you, Steorra," I rasped, pressing my lips to her temple. "Whether the demoness is here or gone, I love you. I will fight for you. And I will not leave you again. Not ever."

"I will burn for you forever," she mumbled into my chest, soaking my skin with her fresh tears. The remnants of my shirt hung draped around her face, both our bodies covered in a heavy coating of ash. Surely the demoness couldn't possibly have survived her flame. Nothing that hot, the way she gave all of herself...

"She has to be gone," I whispered, prayed, *begged*.

"She is." Tifa's voice broke into my thoughts that consumed me.

I spun us around to face the witch and Sebastian. The vampire's pale fade was drawn and closed. Dark eyes met mine, his mouth a tight line. "You know this how?"

"Because I watched. Every moment. Without blinking." Tifa raised her jewel bright eyes to me, but not the witch's gaze was as clouded as pale jade, the skin around her eyes reddened and burned. She stared blindly in my direction, led by my voice alone, I believed. "I did not take my eyes off the event, not even when you combusted. I watched every moment," she repeated without blinking, staring unfocused at some point over my shoulder that I knew she couldn't see. "She is gone. She cannot return."

"Oh Tifa." Ash placed a tentative hand on the other woman's arm. "I am thankful as I am sorry."

The witch turned her face in Ash's direction. "I am not sorry. Now, we know. Now, you are all safe." She smiled and leaned back into Sebastian's arms, closing her eyes as tears ran from the corners.

Sebestian closed his arms around her, watching us over her head. After a moment, he led her away, along the silent row of graves until they disappeared behind a curtain of ash and embers.

"It's over, Steorra." I stroked her hair. "May I take you home?"

She shivered in my arms. "She has burned most of my clothes." A frown decorated her perfect face, despite the dark smudges that marred her cheeks, and the thin scar that ringed her slender throat in a permanent scar. "Wait. You don't have a home."

I smiled. "Let me show you."

EPILOGUE

ASH

I sat beside Dolion in his stone form on the rooftop of an abandoned gothic church built sometime around the early thirteen hundreds situated deep in a French forest that had long forgotten its own name and was at peace. The twisted gargoyle's face warded off evil things and the sun set over the edge of the trees as night set in.

Not that it mattered. My own heat kept us warm.

I hadn't had an incident since the night in the graveyard, and now I had a new line of crypts to discover. The names on some had worn off with time, but on others the dates and family names were still visible. And inside the church, Dolion had kept the lists of everyone buried within the grounds. The taphophile in me was pleased with that treasure. I limited myself to a single name and a single story each day, learning all who were buried in our new home.

Sebastian and Tifa remained in New Orleans. It turned out that a vampire made an excellent bartender. Who knew that the nocturnal hunter had such hidden talents. He listened, he grumped and no one questioned his ability to deal with the security side of the job. Tifa sat at the bar, wrapped in her shawls, never far from where Sebastian worked. We remained in New Orleans until we were sure she was as comfortable as possible and him too and then...

We left. Found our own place and future for once. Because Dolion did what he promised and he took me home.

I stroked his stone form, telling him all about Gregory—I had located five Gregories thus far in our graveyard—of today's story, and everything I'd been able to discern from the monks who once tended the church below us. Like many religious institutions, it had been known by several names. Fortunately, the documents had stayed with the building, and so I was able to piece the histories of the place together.

Soon, my gargoyle would awake. A good thing

too, as though I napped and read and discovered during the day, my nights were full of a different sort of discovery.

A new life grew within me.

For the first time in six thousand years I had more than one reason to exist.

My belly rounded with the creature Dolion placed within me. We knew little about my own creation, my own family, or his. All we did know was that this child would be loved. This child would know everything we did. All of our history and those who came before us. The histories and mistakes we made, the love that was sacrificed so we could find each other.

Soon, my gargoyle would wake and remind me why we loved, and who the man was that I had fallen for. An impossible stone man who helped me find peace and accept the magic inside me. Who helped create the beautiful miracle of new life inside me.

A seed of stone with a heart of pure flame.

THANK YOU SO MUCH FOR READING

Dolion and Ash's story. The SILENT SENTINELS world ends here, and I appreciate the time you have taken in reading through both their world and Sebastian and Gisella's.

Please leave a review. It really matters to authors!

There are more shifters...

Read on for a glimpse into Krampus after he awakes into a world he's not sure about and finds his brand new obsession: a girl who never dates the same man twice in

KRAMPUS' CHRISTMAS BRIDE

KRAMPUS CHRISTMAS BRIDE - SNEAK PEEK

CHAPTER ONE

DEVLIN

I sit across from my date and smile into my coffee mug in a way that brings a pretty strain to her cheeks. The girl—an adult in every sense of the word though still many centuries younger than I am —let me have a second date with her, and that, in her short history, is unheard of.

Just as a Krampus stalker like myself should know.

You see, Tanya Hinson is on the naughty list. *My* naughty list.

Not that she knows it, but watching her flit from date to date in the coffee shop beneath her apartment like her online contacts are her personal flirt bar brews something within me I know I should never let roam free.

Except Christmas is the season I love to hate... and unluckily for her, it's here.

Self control is never something I've worried about, much like my present-tossing brother who exists off the joy people throw into the atmosphere for a few meager days of the year.

My existence absorbs emotion on a much darker scale.

And Christmas week in San Francisco, a full three days until my big bro's big day, is the prime time to screw around and find out. Twins, born of the same soul and split, like a sunbeam and its shadowy accompaniment. Only I'm not irrevocably linked to my sibling. While Saint Nick is out making all the good offspring of humanity happy, I focus on those a little older, and activities a whole lot... filthier.

The old pamphlets that used to send Europe into a flurry about the horned devil terrorizing children were really just me with a little spanking habit and a whole lot of satisfied wives who wouldn't know what true pleasure was if I didn't visit them on an annual basis.

I mean, a Krampus should share the love, and all.

After a while I became tired of being hunted by cuckolded husbands, and the demands of otherwise unsated housewives addicted to my form of pleasure who got to call themselves a princess while they rode my cock once a year. Then humanity fell into a cesspit of wars so entangled with their own egos that I hid away from the world entirely, and chose to terrorize a few otherworldly creatures for the duration.

When I emerged, I found the world changed, though the people were...different.

The housewives came into their own in an age of liberation where moderation no longer matters. Not that it ever did, but now addictions are out in the open for all and sundry to see. Females like my pretty Tanya spread her legs not for a husband but a thick, buzzing stick in a collection of colors that drew her moan just as loudly as my little harem, now long gone, used up and turned to dust.

A part of me likes this new world, the power I've inadvertently collected in my absence, who I can become in its age of technology I've taken steps to understand. And I like the way the girl—*singular*—I choose to stalk teases and flirts and walks away from her dates and returns to her solo existence above the coffee shop with a secret smile on her face that no one is able to decode.

But I know. I watch her come over and over each night until the city disappears for me and I see only her.

Now, so close to Christmas, I know tonight she'll lie alone on her bed, and my time stalking her has come to a point of action. A call to it, like a siren's song.

Her dark hair flips over her shoulder as she watches me through almond eyes, dark and framed with the sort of thick, curled lashes I've always had a soft spot for. Not too made up; she doesn't need extra help to enhance her natural glow. Some angel bestowed that gift upon her long ago. From the way her eyes peer sexily at me through her lashes, she absolutely understands the effect she has on the male of her species. Possibly a few females, too.

Which is her M.O. To peer through those lashes, all wanton and ripe for juicing, right before she whispers *goodnight*. She'll stand and sashay to the stairs hidden away behind a coded lock where her long line of whimpering, salivating dates with their leaking, erect cocks can't follow.

But I can.

One of my favorite pastimes is picking locks. And the best of those are the ones that sit well above ground level, where the facade of safety withers with height.

Finding her in her bed will be fun. Also, the terror in her eye before I put my clawed hand to good use on her stunning behind. A guy has to have hobbies, right? I savor every single one of mine. And I've had an eon to cultivate enough fantasies to fill even this debauched world that runs on a ceaseless stream of instant gratification. But right now...

"I remember you said work was getting boring." Her first date hit all the right notes: what she did for employment without actually telling me where. Her interests, without being specific. The topping she hates on a pizza.

Graphic designer, loves movies but not what sort or which ones, and pineapple heated up sucks, especially next to cheese.

I have to admit, I sympathize with that last. After our first date I ordered my first pizza from a place a few doors down, perched on the rooftop opposite in my full form like a statuesque gargoyle and devoured the lot from my claws, licking each one clean as she worked herself into a frenzy on her bed, all alone.

But not without an audience of one with a back-drop of a starless night.

For the first time she seemed to sense an extra presence and walked afterwards on wobbly legs to the window, toying with the heavy, red drapes that hung like thickest velvet. Tanya stared out at the city moving sluggishly through the cold night when everyone should have been hurrying to warmer places. Then, without a glance in my direction, even when I let the pizza box flutter to the sidewalk below in the hope she'd glance up and see my monstrous form, she pulled the drapes together.

Almost all the way.

That invitation to draw closer is the one I took whether she wanted me to, or not. Because the slim line of muted light let me view the most tantalizing glimpse of curved, plump thighs just right to dig my claws into and split apart before I tasted her center.

She did the job for me, spreading her legs wide as I watched, her fingers digging into the oh so soft flesh, and worked her fingers—four of them, her hands were that small—into her sweetly scented pussy until she gushed with a cry.

Tanya fell asleep with her legs spread wide, her glistening fingers draped across her stomach, and her chest still rising and falling a little faster than normal.

I knew; I checked her regular breathing on both our dates. Which brings me back to the one that, by my count, should be almost over, if she holds to her usual course of action.

"Work is...slow." She sighs, her blouse lifting a little, gifting me the barest glimpse of a slice of her tender belly across the table. Of course, I've seen so much more. Still, the tease is so sweet. I salivate at her effort. "I want something more challenging than ad copy and social media posts. But it pays enough and so...that's what I do."

"Perhaps it's time for a change." I shrug, leaning back in my chair as the conversation in the cafe hit a lull point. This human form itches. My horns ache to burst through and my tail is jammed up my own ass. "People often have more than one occupation these days, it seems."

Tanya watches me with a crinkled brow. "You sound like an old man, yet you look too young for gray hairs."

"Appearances can be deceitful."

Her lips turn down, and her watchful eyes never leave me, much like the way I can't stop seeing her whether she's awake or asleep. "Why do you put it that way?"

"What way?" I toy with my cup, twirling it in quick circles without spilling a drop of the burnt milk and overcooked beans.

"Deceitful. That's not the phrase. Everything about you is..."

Slightly off.

She doesn't need to say it; we both follow her thoughts. And she's right in that gut instinct. If she's smart and varies her habits, it might save her one day.

But not from me.

I reach across the table and clasp her hand like the lovelorn fucker I most certainly am not.

Obssesser, not a lover. I mangle their phrases with pride.

Not a lover tonight, anyway. Right now, I have goals.

Tanya remains seated, though her smile strains. "I'm not very good at second dates."

I consider a moment, not letting her hands go and circle her wrist with my fingers. *Christ, she's small.* So much more fun to break later. "Not true. You just don't go on many."

Her hands leave mine with a sharp tug that only frees her because I let go. From the way her eyes flare as she wraps her arms around herself, she knows it, too.

"Thank you for the coffee, Mister David."

Her eyes skate over me dismissively, but not before they narrow, taking in everything I want her to see and a few things I don't.

"Devlin." I supplied the fake name that appears to fit this form best, knowing she didn't really forget.

"Devlin. Of course," she murmurs.

And she turns, leaving me with a half drunk cappuccino and part of a shared date loaf she never touched.

I don't blame her. The damn stuff tastes like poison.

Her jeans fit perfectly to the curves of her ass as she sashays away without a single glance over her shoulder. There will be no invitation from her tonight, or any other night. Not for me, her date last week, the one tomorrow, or the night after that.

No one ever gets up those stairs or between her pretty legs.

No one ever tastes her, and it's such a loss.

One I intend to change tonight.

Being on my naughty list has perks. And some other things.

Read KRAMPUS' CHRISTMAS BRIDE here

ABOUT THE AUTHOR

Raven Hush writes paranormal & BDSM romance and exists on a diet of red wine and coffee. When she isn't romancing the monster under her bed, she writes contemporary romance and suspense as *USA Today bestselling* author Sofia Aves and kidlit under a not-so-super-secret pen name. Raven has worked with Romance Writers of Australia as Marketing and Events Manager and lives at Romance Cafe Publishing in their Marketing and PR department. She is a stay-at-home mum living near Brisbane, Australia with her three crazies and two German shepherds who like to pose whilst wrestling. Raven writes in her own dragon bookish cave and wrangles her alpacas daily. One day, she might even write about them.

Bookishly stalk Raven:

WEBSITE

AMAZON

BOOKBUB

INSTAGRAM

TWITTER

FACEBOOK

READ RAVEN'S BOOKS

Writing spicy paranormal romance as
RAVEN HUSH

Club Fray
Darkest Desires

Purge

Kidnapped By Claws

Ruin

Shadow Lords
Sinner's End

Heaven's Gate (2026)

Monster Brides
Phoenix's Eternal Flame

Kraken's Vow

Krampus' Christmas Bride

Silent Sentinels Duet
Reflections of Silence
Echoes in the Void

Monsters In New York
Feral Moon Rising (2025)

Writing Romantasy as
SOFIA SHELLEY
Dead Poets Sorority

Writing Reverse Harem Dark Romance as
DOVE PRIEST
Recurve Ridge

Writing Steamy Romance as Sofia Aves
Blue Blooded Brothers
Collision
Politics & Paperwork
Blindsided
Sentinel
Mugshots & Candy Canes
Impact
Reckoning

Red Hart Ranch

Snow on the Range

Siren on the Range

Sundown on the Range

Spirit on the Range

Ash on the Range

Mistletoe on the Range

Forgotten Mountain Man

Gourd Enough To Eat

Texan Devils

Ranger's Wish

Ranger Bedevilled

Ranger's Passion

Ranger's Fury

Ranger's Wrath

Ranger's Storm

Snapdragons & Seductions

Summer with a Ranger

Merry with a Ranger

Playing to Win

Off Boarding

Vicious Slash

Zero Pointer

Off Stage Fling

Rippton Allstars
Crushing It
Glacial Force

Rippton Creatives
Study Games
Make Me, Break Me
Twisted Obsession
Spring Break with a Mafia Prince
A Royally Fake French Menage

Jericho Chimeras
Puck Me Always
Puck My Heart
Puck me Sideways

Z Boys
King
Joker
Hearts
Ace
Mayhem & Mistletoe
Ruski

Fast Track to Love
Speed Trap

Klauss Brothers

Zander

Keegan

Gallo Empire *with Jade Marshall*

Splintered Vows

Fractured Vows

Fierce Vows

Savage Covenant

Rom Coms

She's A Hot Christmas Mess

Boats, Moats and Root Beer Floats

Kidlit writing as
JO SEYSENER

The OCD Elf

Greg and the Egg

writing YA as
JOSS PHOENIX

Alchem Academy

Hide From Us

www.ingramcontent.com/pod-product-compliance
Lightning Source LLC
Chambersburg PA
CBHW031427200626
46814CB00016B/2723